# A CHRISTMAS DUO

**Annie Seaton**

A Christmas Duo

Annie Seaton

Her Christmas Star originally published in

Baby, It's Hot Outside Anthology

Christmas With the Boss

New revised edition September 2019

Annie Seaton

# Her Christmas Star

## Annie Seaton

# Chapter One

Lisa Greer stood in the foyer of the luxury apartment; her head tilted slightly to one side as she listened for any sound from her employer's suite, but only the low hum of the air conditioner broke the silence. Taking a deep breath, a gasp tore from her throat as she turned to the door.

*Deep breath, big mistake.* Her throat was so sore, it hurt to breathe in. That deep breath had just about finished her. Closing her eyes, Lisa waited for the sharp pain to ease before she took another breath. Her head began to spin, and a cold sweat gripped her as the doorknob twisted silently beneath her clammy fingers. The latch let go with a loud click and she froze as the sound reverberated up the hall. She waited, but no sound came from the bedroom suite on the other side of the apartment.

Tasha was resting and had made it very clear she was *not* to be disturbed under any circumstances because she needed her beauty sleep for the pre-Christmas dinner tonight. Apparently, as well as the cast of the movie, all the "who's who" in Sarnia Bay were going to be at the dinner. The small, but exclusive, Sarnia Bay on the north coast of New South Wales had overtaken Byron Bay as the "in" destination for both Australian and international movie stars. Tasha le Clair, her employer of just over a week, had flown in from the UK three months ago to take a role in the movie that was currently being shot at the Bay.

Lisa pulled a face. Beauty sleep to improve her employer's appearance would take more than an hour, she thought uncharitably. Tasha le Clair might have been a beautiful movie star once—a long, *long* time ago—but the years had not been kind to her; the cosmetic work, and the heavy makeup she insisted on, gave her a garish appearance. Arched eyebrows created a permanent look of surprise and her plumped up lips looked ridiculous, especially with her signature ruby-red lipstick. Jagged furrows from a perpetual frown were etched in her forehead and deep lines creased her rouged cheeks. Normally Lisa would not be so critical, but Tasha had not earned her respect. Even though she had given Lisa a job, Tasha le Clair was *not* a nice person.

Hesitating, she bit her lip. It would only take a couple of minutes to run down to the pharmacy across the road; if she didn't get some cold and flu medication to get her through the day and the big night ahead, she wouldn't be able to do her job.

Tasha wouldn't even know she'd left the apartment, but still Lisa hesitated. Her employment conditions had been made very clear; she was *not* to leave the apartment in working hours unless Tasha sent her on a chore.

A languid wave of a wrinkled, bejewelled hand had accompanied the command. 'My last PA spent most of the day in the coffee shop in the foyer trying to get the attention of the movie stars. Stupid girl,' Tasha had said. 'As if they would have looked at her! Although she *was* better looking than you. You're quite the plain Jane, aren't you, Lisa? Gaunt is the word I'd use.'

*Yes, I am.* Lisa knew she didn't meet the standard of the beautiful people of the movie world, or the buxom beach babe set that her ex had become enamoured with when they had stopped at the Bay last month. She knew she was too short—petite— her Scottish nan had said kindly when Lisa had complained about her height one day. Her figure was boyish, and her green eyes were too big for her small face. Her ex's *new* woman had the hourglass figure, the fake boobs, the fake tan and the long blonde hair—bleached.

Guy had been a mistake from day one. The only thing he'd left her with had been his blasted flu germs. The worst thing was, he'd taken off in the van with all her possessions, including her wallet and visa card *and* he knew her pin number. By the time Lisa got to the bank, her account had been cleaned out. All she had to her name was a hundred dollars she'd put in her pocket when she'd left the van to work at the ice cream shop where she'd picked up a job for a week while he surfed. That was supposed to supplement their income as they'd travelled. The only other thing she had was her iPad that she'd taken to work so she could read in her break.

If Guy hadn't taken off with everything, Lisa knew she wouldn't have been so bitchy about Coco, his new woman—fake name too, of course.

Good riddance to him. Cheap travel had been the enticement rather than Guy himself; his attraction had worn off quickly, and Lisa had moved out of the van to sleep in the swag after they'd been travelling only a week. Guy had some strange sexual tastes. Tastes she did not want to be a party to.

*You always make poor choices, gel,* Nan would have said. That's where her lily-white skin and red hair came from. From Nan, and the Scottish highland connection. It might look good on Jamie Fraser, but on short and skinny Lisa Greer? No way.

Guy had told her she was too scrawny the few nights they had spent in the same bed.

*Lowlife.* Never again would she trust a man.

Lisa had nodded when Tasha had stared at her; however, a reply to Tasha's observations was not expected. One did *not* engage in conversation with the star. Lisa's role as the personal assistant of Tasha le Clair had been made extremely clear to her.

As crazy as the conditions were for a 24/7 live-in personal assistant, Lisa followed the rules. This job with the aging movie star was all she had. She *needed* it; she had no money, no car, nowhere to live, and nowhere to go. She'd spent most of the hundred dollars on food, and a room for two nights at the backpacker hostel. She was due back in Cairns at the beginning of March to start her childcare course, but until then, she had to support herself and find somewhere to live.

Since Nan had passed last June, Lisa had no one left close to her. No one she could tell her hopes, her dreams, her fears. There'd been a couple of school friends in Cairns, but they'd moved on with their new lives with partners and kids. Maybe she wouldn't even go back to Cairns and start the course; she could try elsewhere once she was on her feet.

Frustration filled Lisa; if she was going to make it through the night, and Tasha's demands, she'd have to take the risk and leave the apartment now. If she didn't get some medication into her system, she'd be no use helping get Tasha ready for the dinner tonight, and she'd probably lose her job anyway. Patting her jeans pocket, she checked her last ten-dollar note was there. It crinkled beneath her fingers and before she could change her mind, she pulled the door open.

'Where the hell do you think you're going?'

Lisa spun around, her head spinning from the sudden movement. Tasha was beside her, her dark eyes glittering with anger, her sullen mouth turned down more than usual.

'I thought I heard someone at the door. I was just checking.' Lisa's voice rasped in her raw throat. 'I was trying not to wake you.'

Tasha lunged forward and her fingers pressed into the skin of Lisa's wrist. 'Get back in here, you ugly little bitch. You're lying, the buzzer didn't sound. No one can get up here without the concierge checking first.'

A deep voice came from behind Lisa, and her heart thudded so hard, she felt faint.

'I'm sorry I've woken you, Tasha. The concierge let me come up. He knew you wouldn't mind seeing me.'

Tasha let go of Lisa's arm and stepped back into the dark hall. Another rule was that the drapes always remained closed, despite the glorious ocean views from every room.

'Oh, *daahling* Julien,' she said. 'Do come in, but you'll have to give me five minutes to freshen up.' She turned to Lisa and the sweet smile disappeared instantly. '*You* go down to the delicatessen and get some more of that *pate de fois gras* I served last night, and some grapes.' Her smile reappeared as she turned back to the man at the door. 'You missed such a good night, *daahling*. We missed you.' The put-on pout made the red lips appear even more grotesque.

*A bit like those clowns at the circus.* Lisa smothered a smile and cleared her throat, and her voice was husky as she asked quietly, 'Do you have an account at the delicatessen, Tasha?'

'No. *You* pay for it. Keep the docket and I'll fix you up when you get paid at the end of the month.'

Lisa straightened her shoulders and her throat burned as she swallowed. 'I don't have any cash.'

'Use your card.'

The burning moved up to Lisa's cheeks as humiliation washed over her. 'I don't have a card,' she said quietly.

'Oh, for God's sake!' Tasha rolled her eyes. 'Julien, do you have trouble getting competent staff in Australia? I knew I should have brought my

11

wonderful Eric over with me from London. *This* person is the seventh Australian PA I've had in three months. They still have the convict work ethic in the Antipodes, I'm sure. Reminds me of that Captain Cook movie I starred in.' Tasha's plummy English tone was at odds with the vitriol in her tone. 'Honestly, *daahling*, it makes my life here almost unbearable. Knowing I'm starring with you in *Our Lost Love* is the only reason I've stayed Down Under.'

Lisa gritted her teeth, fighting back the urge to tell Tasha Le Clair exactly what she thought of her. Everyone on the set, and probably everyone in Sarnia Bay would cheer when she left. They'd probably have a party. When the aging star had arrived to work on the movie—playing a secondary role—word of her difficult reputation had quickly spread through the town. If Lisa hadn't been desperate, she wouldn't have even considered applying for the PA position; Tasha le Clair was a bitch of the first order.

'Allow me to assist, *ma chère*.' The voice from behind her was deep, smooth and accented.

Lisa had forgotten about the man at the door and as she turned, her gaze landed on his hands as he took his wallet from his pocket and pulled out a hundred dollar note.

Long, elegant fingers brushed hers as he

12

handed the note to Lisa before she lifted her gaze to meet his eyes.

Her head spun again and her throat dried.

Oh my God!

*Julien*? She should have picked up on that straight away, but her head was like cottonwool today.

My God, *Julien Joubert. Her idol. Her hero. The man who had starred in her erotic dreams all week.*

Smouldering blue eyes held hers and Lisa found it impossible to drag her gaze away.

Smouldering, *sexy*, deep-blue eyes fringed with lush dark lashes, eyes that had held Lisa entranced while she had binge-watched every one of his movies in the past week on Tasha's huge television when the old cow went out for dinner, and then on her own iPad when her employer came home and retired for the night.

His lips lifted in a smile and it was as though she was the only woman in the world. The same smile she'd swooned over night after night. Julien Joubert in his many roles had been her escape from the shock of Guy taking her money.

*Homeless and destitute*. When she was immersed in a Julien Joubert movie Lisa could kid herself everything was okay, and now, here he was, standing beside her. Hell, he was standing so close she could feel the warmth of his skin.

'Th . . . th . . . thank you,' she stammered. 'I'll bring the change back to you straight away.'

'Don't worry about it. Use it to buy yourself something nice, *ma chère*.' The note of sympathy in the star's gorgeous voice cheered Lisa as he waved a dismissive hand, and she took off down the fire stairs, her legs shaking like jelly.

And they weren't shaking because of her flu.

# Chapter Two

When the beautiful PA left, Julien managed to keep his expression bland as he turned to Tasha Le Clair. Her eyes narrowed, and he knew immediately she hadn't appreciated him giving money to her assistant. Staff didn't stay with her long, and he well knew her reputation. He'd witnessed firsthand how badly Tasha treated her staff, but *la garce* always got away with it, because she was a brilliant award-winning actress with a stellar reputation, and people wanted to be associated with her. He hadn't been at all surprised when he'd heard that she'd won the role of the family matriarch in *Our Lost Love*. Unsurprised, but that didn't mean he had to be happy about working with her.

Julien was especially not happy about having to put up with her off the set. He had worked with some prima donnas, but he'd never worked with anyone as demanding as Tasha. On set she was the consummate professional, but socially, *mon Dieu*, she was horrendous.

'Look, mate,' Gaz Hermann, the Australian producer, had taken Julien aside after the first production meeting before Tasha arrived. 'Butter her up and we'll all be sweet.'

'*Moi?* Butter her up?' He'd stared at the eccentric producer with the long grey beard and ponytail. 'What is this *sweet*?'

'You know what I mean. We'll all be happy. Tasha likes a drink or three. She likes company and most of all, she needs to have a good-looking man at her side. That's your job until we get her scenes shot and she goes back to London. *Capiche*?'

Julien stared at him for a moment before he nodded. '*Capiche*. But, on my terms.'

So here he was providing a buffer for the producer, the director, and the rest of the crew. Keeping Tasha le Clair *sweet*. But maybe she wouldn't be so sweet after he talked to her this afternoon.

'I'll pour us a drink while you freshen up, Tasha.'

'Thank you, darling. I fancy a *Prosecco*.' A cloud of cloying perfume surrounded him as she brushed a kiss on each of his cheeks. 'You're such a good boy, Julien. I'm so pleased you came to see me today. I couldn't wait until tonight. Where were you last night?' There was an edge to her voice.

'I had an unexpected interruption. I'll take our drinks out to the balcony, and tell you all about it when you've freshened up.'

'I'll be very quick. I feel so much better now that you're here. I was feeling quite stressed.'

No wonder she was feeling stressed; the apartment was dark, musty and claustrophobic. After Tasha had closed her bedroom door Julien opened the velvet drapes, flooding the room with sunlight, and then unlocked the door to the main balcony overlooking the water. He crossed to the bar and poured a *Prosecco* for her and filled a second champagne flute with soda water for himself; he needed to keep his wits about him for more than one reason today.

With a sigh, he walked out to the balcony and stared out over the white-capped waves. A car horn blared four floors below and as he looked down, Tasha's tiny PA came out of the pharmacy and hurried along the street to the delicatessen.

*Poor young woman.* She looked barely old enough to be working, let alone putting up with someone like Tasha le Clair. She must have a bit of sense because she'd lasted over a week; longer than the other—how many had Tasha said—seven? A couple of weeks ago Julien had first noticed the girl working at the ice-cream shop; his attention had been caught by her stunning eyes. Huge green eyes set in a pretty face; she could have played one of the street urchins in the movie he'd just finished in Italy. A delicate face with high cheekbones, and flawless skin so fair it was almost transparent. Julien had found himself paying more attention to her prettiness than was wise with Tasha looking on.

The door slid open behind him and he turned. Tasha wore a huge sun hat and enormous sunglasses covered half her face.

'Thank you, *daahling,*' she twittered, her expression impossible to read as he passed her the crystal flute. 'That Lisa girl stresses me. I might have to let her go, I think. I know she was sneaking out.' Her eyes narrowed. 'She wasn't going to meet you, was she?'

Julien raised his eyebrows and pulled out one of the padded wrought iron chairs for her. 'No, of course not. I came to see you.'

Tasha sat, her shoulders straight and her gaze intense.

'You look tired, sweetheart. Were you out late last night?'

A frisson of annoyance skittered through him. She might be an established star, and he had been given the job of keeping her "sweet" but what he did in his own time was none of her business. 'I had to go up to Brisbane.'

Tasha looked at him and he knew she was waiting for his explanation, but he lifted his glass of soda water and drained it before placing it on the table.

'I can only stay a short while. I came over to tell you that I won't be able to escort you to the dinner tonight.'

'What?' The painted lips pursed. 'Why ever not?'

'I have another commitment, and I'll be late arriving, so I'll see you at the table. I may even miss the dinner, but I will most probably be there afterwards. Gaz said he will meet you at the door and escort you to our table.'

'What other commitment?' Her voice was dangerously quiet.

Julien's temper began a slow burn. 'I'll arrive about nine.'

'What commitment? That is simply not good enough, Julien. I do not want Gaz to escort me.' Tasha slammed her glass onto the glass table and the stem snapped. She threw the remainder of the glass and its contents onto the tiled floor of the balcony. 'You will be here at seven.'

'No. That is impossible, Tasha.'

'How dare you! You expect me to turn up unaccompanied, like a . . . like a . . . washed-up star!' She stood and stamped her foot. 'If you can't take me, I shall go alone.'

Julien shook his head, and his shrug was very Gallic. He kept his expression and voice light as he turned to the door. He had more problems to worry about than the histrionics of a difficult movie star. *'C'est la vie,* Tasha. I will see you at our table at nine.'

'You're trying to ruin my Christmas. Get out!' she screeched.

He did so.

*With great pleasure.*

# Chapter Three

'I really do think you need to see a doctor, miss.'

Lisa shook her head as the grey-haired pharmacist frowned at her over his spectacles.

'I just need some paracetamol and some cold and flu tablets please.' As her fingers closed over the money in her pocket, a wave of dizziness left Lisa feeling weak and vague. 'Please, I'm in a hurry. I have to get back to work as quickly as I can.'

'You shouldn't be working. You should be in bed. This is a very nasty summer flu that's doing the rounds at the Bay.' The elderly man shook his head and took a box of paracetamol and another packet from the shelf behind the counter. 'You take two paracetamol every four hours, stay in bed and drink plenty of fluids.'

She nodded and her head pounded harder. For a few seconds she thought she was going to throw up. 'I will. Thank you.'

*Stay in bed? I wish.*

'And don't mix them with the night flu tablets, or they'll knock you out. Take two of those at bedtime without the paracetamol.' As Lisa watched, the man's head seemed to recede and then grow bigger. His eyes joined in a blur and he looked like an alien in one of those sci fi movies Guy had loved.

She blinked, took another deep breath that seared her throat and then fought the faintness that threatened. 'I won't.'

'If you get any worse, please present to Emergency at the local hospital. The medical clinics will be closed for the weekend. They'll open Monday and then close again on Christmas and Boxing Days. Take these to the front counter. Mandy will serve you.'

'Thank you,' Lisa whispered as he pushed the two boxes over the dispensary counter. *Christmas? So close?* With Guy taking off, she'd lost track of the days.

At the front counter, the pharmacy assistant rang up the total. 'Fifteen dollars and sixty cents, thank you. Will that be card or cash?' the young girl asked as she slipped the two boxes into a brown paper bag stamped with the name of the pharmacy.

Lisa hesitated as she went to pass the ten dollars over. *Oh, damn. Maybe I should just get the cold and flu tablets?*

But Julien Joubert had told her to buy herself something nice. She could use his money for the five dollars sixty she was short, and then pay him back when Tasha paid her on Christmas Eve.

Lisa added the hundred dollar note to her ten and pushed them both across the counter. 'Please take the five dollars sixty from the hundred.' Despite her head spinning, she could still work that out.

The young girl looked at her with concern as she handed over the change. 'Do you have someone to drive you home? You're awfully pale.'

'I'm in the apartments across the road from the beach. It's not far.'

'Okay, I hope you feel better soon. Horrible to be sick for Christmas.'

Lisa nodded and left the pharmacy and headed to the delicatessen two doors down Sarnia Way. It didn't take long to complete the purchase, and it was only a couple of minutes more before she'd taken the elevator up and was back in the foyer outside the apartment. She pushed open the front door and slipped inside quietly. Low voices came from the balcony as she put the food in the fridge, filled a glass with water and took two of the paracetamol capsules.

As she stood at the window looking at the

sea—the only window in the apartment without drapes—Tasha's voice screeched from outside.

'How dare you!'

Julien's voice was quiet, and Lisa strained to hear what he was saying; her ears were blocked but she had no problem hearing Tasha's abuse.

'You're trying to ruin my Christmas. Get out!'

Footsteps crossed the tiled foyer, and the front door opened and closed.

'Lisa! Bring me a gin and tonic, girl. Now!'

##

It took an hour, and four gin and tonics before Lisa was able to calm her employer down. At least the paracetamol had kicked in; her own headache had eased, and her throat was not as sore as it had been before she'd taken the medication.

'Do you think you should have a lie down?' Lisa suggested quietly as Tasha slammed the empty glass on the marble coffee table for the fourth time and slumped back on the sofa, placing her other hand in a dramatic gesture over her face.

For a moment, Lisa felt a little sorry for the older woman; Julien Joubert had obviously said something to upset her, but Lisa soon shrugged it off. She was well used to Tasha's mercurial moods. Julien would likely be her best friend again before the night was out. 'You don't want to be tired for

24

the dinner.'

'No, I must look my best. Especially after that awful Frenchman let me down. How dare he!' Her voice was shrill again, but Lisa knew better than to comment.

'While you rest, I'll lay your clothes out and run a bubble bath for you. Have you decided on the red or the silver evening dress?'

'The red. Call me when the bath is ready.' Tasha stood, put the back of her hand against her forehead in another melodramatic gesture and let out an exaggerated sigh. 'I shall make sure Julien never works in the industry again. Gaz will listen to me!'

Lisa nodded and left her employer muttering. She went to the bathroom and turned the taps on over the huge sunken bath set in the middle of the floor.

*Sorry, sweetheart*, she thought, as she sprinkled dried rose petals beneath the gushing water and lit the tealight candles in the crystal holders set in the wide rim of the bath. *You've got no chance. He's way more famous than you are. And much easier on the eye.*

It would be an interesting battle, but one that Lisa didn't need to be a part of. All she wanted was a quiet and peaceful Christmas and enough money to get back to Cairns.

Back to the city where Nan was buried and where she could make a fresh start.

## 

Tasha left the apartment just after six-thirty in a cloud of *Giorgio* perfume and silver rippling fabric; she'd changed her mind three times before settling on the silver dress.

'It doesn't matter what I look like,' she bitched, playing the martyr. 'I am going to the ball by myself. Like Cinderella.' She'd made Lisa call the producer to say he was *not* to pick her up.

Lisa had smiled when she'd heard the relief in Gaz's reply. 'Sweet, Lisa. Thanks, love.'

As soon as the door shut behind Tasha, Lisa watched from the balcony, ensuring her employer exited the foyer of the apartment and crossed the road to the Sarnia Premium Hotel.

With a deep sigh of relief she collapsed onto the sofa, too weak to even get herself a glass of water. Eventually she roused herself when thirst chased her into the kitchen. As she stood at the sink, she tried to remember what the pharmacist had said, but his words eluded her, so she took two more paracetamol plus two of the cold and flu tablets.

She could doze until midnight. Tasha wouldn't be in early. When there were people around to suck up to her and pander to her ego, she would stay out until all hours. On those nights, this job did have its good points for Lisa. It made up for the long days that she was expected to be by Tasha's side on the set. It had been just over a week since she'd begun working for her, but already she'd found the days on the movie set absolutely boring. So much for the glamour of being in the movies.

With a tired smile, Lisa changed into a pair of comfy trackies, grabbed a soft mink blanket, turned on the Smart TV, and found her favourite Julien Joubert movie on Netflix. Her throat was too sore to think about food so she refilled her glass with iced water to sip on as she watched. Pulling out her phone, she set the alarm for ten-thirty p.m. That would give her plenty of time to cover her tracks before her employer came home. There must be no sign of her having used Tasha's sofa or television. That was a sackable offence, according to the silly cow.

Settling into the soft couch, Lisa pulled the blanket up to her chin, pressed play and began to watch the movie. Her eyelids were heavy, and she tried desperately to fight sleep as the movie played. Snuggling into the sofa, she smiled, closing her eyes and soon Julien was holding her face gently between his hands as his lips hovered over hers. She arched against him, and he lowered his hands slipping the thin straps of her silk top over her

27

shoulders and she sighed as the whisper of the silk brushed over her erect nipples.

His lips traced a warm path down her neck and she giggled as he nipped playfully at her shoulder, and then continued the slow and tortuous journey down to her breasts.

'You are so beautiful, Lisa.' His voice sent hot sparks of desire tingling between her legs and she reached down and brushed her fingers lightly over his erection, marvelling that she, plain Lisa Greer, had had that effect on Julien Joubert. Moving her head up again she let her fingertips lightly brush his bare stomach.

*When did he take his clothes off?*

With a deep groan, Julien lifted his head and played his tongue along her bottom lip and when Lisa opened her mouth to speak, he pressed his mouth against her lips. His moist tongue outlined them and when she tried to speak again, he put his finger against her mouth.

'We have no need for words,' he murmured. 'Let me show you instead.' Without seeming to move, Lisa was now lying beneath him. The rough hair on his thighs pressed against her bare legs.

'Now, let me show you all the ways I can pleasure you. We have all night.'

Lisa tried to protest that they didn't, but the words wouldn't come. They didn't have all night;

Tasha would be home soon.

Julien lowered his head again and traced lazy circles around her peaked nipples with his tongue. Lisa gasped as he ran his hand down her stomach, and then across her hips before his fingers brushed across her swollen nub. Heat ran through her and a moan broke from her lips when he increased the pressure and slipped one finger inside her. Every rational thought slid from her brain as she responded instantly to his touch.

Her phone alarm drowned out Julien's whispers as his fingers worked magic. Lisa tried to hold onto the feeling as her eyes opened sluggishly.

She was alone on the sofa; it was all a dream, but what a wonderful dream. She frowned as the loud noise continued.

*Where the hell was it?*

Lisa panicked, wondering how long she'd been asleep. She jumped up, tripped on the blanket, grabbed for the phone and banged her knee on the marble coffee table.

'Shit, shit, shit.' As she jumped around the room clutching her phone, she realised it wasn't the alarm on her phone buzzing. She'd actually only been asleep for about half an hour. The phone was *ringing*, and it was Tasha.

'Double shit.' She stabbed at the answer button. 'Hello.' Her voice came out as a husky croak. She cleared her throat and then coughed and then tried again. 'Hello, this is Lisa.'

'Where are you and what the hell are you doing?' Tasha's voice was hard. 'Why did it take you so long to answer?'

'Um, I was in the bathroom,' Lisa lied.

'You are to go into my bedroom *now*, and get my red lipstick and my perfume off the dresser. Did you hear me? *Now*. Come over to the ballroom in the hotel and bring them straight to me.'

Lisa cleared her throat and nodded.

'Did you hear me?'

'Yes. The red lipstick and your perfume to the hotel.'

'Now. You have five minutes, or you'll have no job.'

The call disconnected and Lisa widened her eyes in horror. She wouldn't have time to get changed. She hit the power button on the television, quickly folded the blanket and put it back into the cupboard, and ran into Tasha's room.

*Bloody hell.* Red lipstick? Which one? There were about twenty red lipsticks on the dressing table. She scooped them all into a makeup bag and picked up the atomiser of perfume Thank God, that was easy. Tasha only wore *Giorgio*.

Slipping her feet into the thongs by the door, Lisa grabbed her key and raced down the hall to the elevator. Her mouth dried as she realised it was at the ground floor and would take the best part of a minute to come up to the fourth floor.

Finally, the bell dinged and clutching the makeup bag she jumped in and pressed the ground floor button. Slowly the elevator descended and when the doors opened, she sprang out and ran through the foyer, dodged cars on the busy road, and arrived in the foyer of the luxury hotel with half a minute to spare. She raced across to the concierge, and her words were garbled; it hurt to breathe when she spoke to him.

'Can you please'—deep searing breath—'give this to Miss le Clair for me?'

He shook his head. 'No, she specifically asked me to ensure that you take it in to her.'

Lisa was horrified. 'But I can't—'

'She's waiting for you at the table. You'd better hurry, love. She's not happy.' He pulled a face at her.

Lisa groaned. She was damned if she did, and damned if she didn't.

With a final look down at her grey trackies, thongs and wrinkled T-shirt, she sighed and pushed open the door to the ballroom. Relief flooded through her as she stepped into the room. Thank God, the room was dimly lit and the spotlight was on the stage, directed at the entertainer who had the crowd laughing at his commentary.

Biting her lip, Lisa scanned the room, and spotted Tasha at one of the front tables to the side of the stage. Pressing herself against the wall, Lisa quickly skirted the room until she reached Tasha's table. She bent double and tried to make herself as inconspicuous as possible as she crouched beside her employer. 'Your lipstick and your perfume are in the bag.' Lisa pushed the cosmetic bag across the table and turned to make her escape.

'And I'm supposed to carry that bag around all night? For God's sake, girl, what were you thinking?' Tasha sat straight and grabbed Lisa's hand.

'I didn't know which lipstick you wanted. Just take the one you want and the atomiser, and I'll take the bag back with me,' Lisa whispered desperately.

'*You're* telling me what to do? How dare you. Next thing you'll want to be in the movie, I expect!'

Lisa flinched. Her wrist was still bruised from this afternoon. 'No. Just tell me what you want, and *I'll* do it.'

Before Tasha could reply, there was a drum roll, and the table was suddenly lit by a spotlight that landed directly on Lisa crouched at the corner of the table. Her eyes widened and her heart thudded as she was bathed in the bright light and the situation took a turn for the worse.

'Tonight, the Sarnia Premium would like to welcome our special guest, the one and only Tasha le Clair.'

Lisa tried to stand and fade into the darkness against the wall, but she was pinned in the spotlight, not to mention in Tasha's vicious grip. As she looked down, the spotlight illuminated her white T-shirt and the dark stain where Tasha's hair dye had marked it when she had touched up Tasha's roots in the bathroom this afternoon. The red colour, the same as Tasha's hair, stood out like a beacon.

Eventually, the spotlight and the entertainer's attention moved to the next table, but Tasha's hand was still gripping her wrist, her long false fingernails breaking Lisa's skin.

'Come with me,' she said coldly. 'Now.'

'Where to?' Lisa tried to tug away, but with no luck. As she did her best to move further back, she looked up and her heartbeat ramped up even more. Julien Joubert was sitting at the table watching the whole interaction. Lisa froze; she had never, ever been so embarrassed in her whole life. All she could think of was the feeling of his body against hers. Her dream had been so real.

He was surrounded by beautifully made-up women in evening clothes; here she was, dressed in a pair of track pants and a stained T-shirt, her nose red, and her hair tousled. Tears stung her eyes and she barely heard Tasha's next words. All Lisa wanted was for the floor to open and swallow her.

*Anything* would be preferable to being embarrassed in front of this crowd of beautiful people. Maybe she should just faint and be carried out, and then she would be unaware of the humiliation.

'To the restroom where I can tell you a few home truths, you stupid girl. You have just lost your job.'

Lisa's head spun, but her temper fired. It was too late to worry about the job; she could tell it was too late to save that. And she didn't want to save it anyway. Working for this old bitch was just too stressful. Even if it meant sleeping on the beach.

'No. I *won't* come with you. There is no point, Tasha. You are impossible to please, and you are impossible to work for. Thank you for terminating my position. Make up my pay, and I'll move on.' Her words were full of false bravado, but the thought of being further humiliated in public spurred her on.

*Move on?* She had nowhere to move on to. 'I'll go back to the apartment, pack and leave tonight, and then I'll come by and collect what you owe me in the morning.'

Her wrist burned where Tasha's fingernails still pressed into her skin.

'I owe you nothing. You have not fulfilled your contract.' The whisper was low and as vicious as her grip.

Horror filled Lisa. She had no money left. She owed Julien Joubert five dollars and sixty cents, and she had no one to bail her out. Her mouth dried and her head spun, but worst of all the pressure on her wrist increased and as she looked down, blood trickled from where Tasha's fingernails had broken her skin.

'You will pay me. Let go of me,' she said quietly.

At the same time, Julien rose from his seat.

'Tasha.' His voice held a warning note. 'Let go of Lisa now, or you'll find yourself up on an assault charge. There are enough witnesses to back your assistant.'

It seemed as though the entire ballroom turned and stared as Tasha's angry scream rang out. It was embarrassing, but she let Lisa go.

All Lisa wanted was to get out of this ballroom, where so many people—and Julien Joubert—had witnessed her humiliation. She put her head down and ran for the door, not paying any heed to the deep voice calling after her, as she prayed there were no cameras recording her flight.

She could just see her face plastered all over a trashy magazine in the supermarket.

'Lisa, wait.'

All she wanted to do was to get out of here, gather up her small bag of belongings and leave. Where she would go, she had no idea, but she wasn't going to worry about that right now. She had to get away.

Lisa pushed open the door of the ballroom, ran across the foyer and through the automatic doors onto the dark street. Putting her head down, and not taking any heed of her surroundings as she ran across the road, she wasn't aware of anything until a horn blared. She put a hand to her face as headlights blinded her, tyres screeched and then something hard knocked into her side. Her arms floundered as she tried to keep her balance, but her legs went from under her. The last thing Lisa was aware of as she nosedived towards the kerb was Julien Joubert running to her, his mouth opened wide as he yelled her name.

# Chapter Four

'*Arrête!* Stop!' Julien took off as he saw the headlights from the car approaching too fast. Lisa raced for the road, but she didn't slow in her mad rush to get away. He had been watching the interaction at the table, and anger had filled him when Tasha treated her so badly. It was obvious from the abject desperation on the younger woman's face that Tasha was being her usually bitchy self.

*Or worse.*

It seemed the prettier her assistant was, the worse Tasha treated them. She might be a brilliant actress, but she was a strange—and very nasty—woman.

And this newest PA—Lisa—was more than pretty; she was beautiful. Julien was sure she didn't remember him, but he'd seen her around town a few times before she'd started working for Tasha. And he'd found it hard to look away; she had an elfin quality that was very attractive.

'You are impossible to please, and you are impossible to work for. Make up my pay, and I'll move on.' Lisa words had been loud and clear, and there were a few sympathetic glances, and low murmurs sent her way from around the table. After a few more words that he couldn't hear over the background noise, the young woman ran from the ballroom.

Julien followed Lisa to the door as she'd rushed out, and now his blood turned to ice as she turned and looked at him before the car hit her. The driver veered away at the last minute, the low-slung sports car just clipping her side. Time seemed to go in slow motion as she lifted her arms, obviously trying to regain her balance but to no avail. Horror filled him as she landed on the hard road. Julien fought for calm as he ran over.

The driver of the sports car pulled over and jumped out, his face white. 'Oh my God, she just ran out in front of me. I didn't see her coming. Man, I had no chance of stopping. Is she dead? Tell me I haven't killed her.'

Lisa was lying on her stomach and Julien caught his breath as she pushed herself up on her hands and looked around. One side of her face was slightly grazed, and her chin was bleeding. 'I'm not dead.'

He crouched down and gently put his hand on her back. 'Lie still, Lisa. Before you move, we need to make sure you haven't broken any bones.' Turning to the distraught young man, he spoke firmly. 'Please call emergency and ask for an ambulance. Do you know the number?'

'Yes, triple zero.'

'Good. Call now.'

As the young man called for help, Lisa tried to sit up, but Julien applied gentle pressure to her shoulders. He hadn't realised how thin she was until he touched her; her bones felt fragile beneath his hands. 'Do not move, *ma chère*. Are you in pain?'

She lay back down, closing her eyes and resting her chin on folded arms. 'No, I'm just very embarrassed. I have made a fool of Tasha.'

'No, do not think that. It was no blame of yours. She can take responsibility for the state you were in.' In his stress, Julien struggled to find the English words he wanted. 'But that is enough. We will worry about that later. First, we must check you are not badly *blessé.*'

'I am a long way from blessed,' she said quietly and the sadness in her voice tugged at his heart.

'*Non. Blessé.* Injured, I mean.'

39

'I told you, I am not hurt. I saved myself with my hands. My cheek scraped the gutter as I landed and I hit my chin on the road, but that is all. Nothing is broken, and I just want to go home.' She lifted her head again. Her eyes flew open, and her lip quivered. 'But I have nowhere to go.'

'Don't you worry about that. We will get something arranged for you as soon as *le médecin* has checked you.'

'Please let me sit up. Honestly, I am *not* hurt. Only my pride.'

'The ambulance is on the way. And the police,' the young driver said glumly.

'Are you sure you are not hurt? There is no pain in your arms or legs or your back? No numbness? Your head, does it ache?'

'I am fine.' Determination and anger filled her voice. 'If you won't help me up, I'll roll over and get up by myself.' The firmness of her tone reassured him.

'*Très bien*. I am not happy about moving you, but if you are insistent, we will do it my way.' Julien crouched closer, gently touched her hip with one hand, and half-rolled her to one side before scooping his arms beneath her slim body. He stood in one swift movement. Her head rested against his shoulder, and her eyes were wide as she stared up at him.

'Oh, why did it have to be you?' she asked.

\*\*\*

Lisa didn't know what to do or say, or how to stop the confusion of feelings that raged through her. Julien's hands—my God, *Julien Joubert* was cradling her against him—were warm against her bare back where her T-shirt had ridden up, but goosebumps ran down her spine at the same time. His hands felt the same as they had in her dream.

*Oh God, don't move. Don't respond*, she told herself as the same tingling sparks ran through her. She felt lightheaded, but knew it had nothing to do with any injury. She hadn't hit her head when she fell—although she was shaking from the shock of the accident—but her faintness was more to do with the man who was holding her.

Only a short time ago, she had been dreaming about being in Julien Joubert's arms, and now she was. But not in the sexy clinch she'd dreamed of. Instead they were in the main street of Sarnia Bay in full view of a growing crowd of onlookers. She drew in a gasp as he stepped into the pool of light from the streetlight, and she saw the blood dripping slowly from her chin onto his white silk shirt. A camera flash lit the darkness.

'Oh, God,' Lisa moaned.

'Where does it hurt? Please give us some space.' His voice was commanding, and the crowd parted as he walked over to a seat on the beach side of the road. Lisa turned her face into his shoulder, hoping no one recognised her, and that her face wasn't in the photo.

The smell of Julien's aftershave, the warmth of his skin and his calm voice soothed her as she closed her eyes.

# Chapter Five

'Will you take her to the hospital?' Julien asked.

Once the paramedics had examined Lisa, and were satisfied there was no head injury, broken bones or injured back, they cleaned the graze on her cheek, and put a strip on her chin to hold the small cut closed.

The male paramedic shook his head in answer to Julien. 'No, mate. She appears not to be injured. If there is any headache or vomiting, attend the hospital.' He looked at Lisa. 'You were a very lucky girl. Go home and get a good night's sleep. Apart from being stiff and a bit sore, you should be as right as rain in the morning.'

Concern filled Julien. She had been very quiet, answering their questions with a simple yes or no, and refusing to look at him. He had also felt her shaking when he held her as they had waited for the ambulance to arrive.

The police had several witnesses and, to the driver's relief, they had been satisfied that the young man had not been at fault. He'd been breathalysed and had been clear.

Julien had been unimpressed when the policewoman had been short with Lisa.

'Next time look before you run out onto the road.' He was sure they thought she was a vagrant or worse; he had seen the look the two young constables had exchanged as they had looked at Lisa's stained clothes and unkempt appearance.

'Have you drunk any alcohol tonight?'

'No.'

'Drugs?'

'Yes,' she said shortly.

Julien stared at her, disappointment filling him until Lisa continued. 'Four paracetamol capsules and two cold and flu tablets. I have the flu.'

'Fair enough.' They climbed into their car and he was relieved when they drove off.

The young driver had stayed with them, and he finally wrote his number on a piece of scrap paper and handed it to Lisa. 'Let me know how you go, and I'll take you out for a drink one night. I feel bad about hitting you.'

Julien frowned. Not if he had any say, would that happen.

44

As the ambulance and the sports car drove away, Lisa stood and sighed. 'I guess I'm going to have to wait for Tasha to come home so I can get in. The concierge will have left and in the rush, I forgot my key to her apartment.' Again, she refused to meet his eye. 'Thank you for taking care of me. I'll be fine here until she leaves the dinner.'

'*Mon Dieu!* What sort of man do you think I am to consider leaving you here alone?'

Lisa shook her head but still didn't look at him. Julien reached for her hand—her skin was hot to the touch—and led her over to the seat where they had waited for the ambulance.

'You are not being truthful with me, Lisa. I heard you quit your job, and I don't blame you. Tasha le Clair does not deserve a faithful employee like you. I saw you today and tonight pandering to her every whim when you were unwell and doing it with grace and a smile on your face. You are a good person.'

Finally, she lifted her face to his, and tears welled in her eyes. 'Until I yelled at her tonight and quit.' She pulled a face. 'That was a very stupid thing to do.'

'No. It was a very brave thing to do, and one we should all take a lesson from. Everyone on the set has pandered to that old woman for too long, and I, for one, will not do it anymore. Not after I have seen how she has treated you. Now, I will drive you to your home, and tomorrow I will accompany you to the apartment to get your wages and your things.' A single tear spilled down her cheek, and Julien fought the urge to take her in his arms. He was never this soft with women and knew how to be immune to tears, but the events of the last three weeks, and the delivery that arrived at Brisbane International Airport had left his emotions raw. 'Are you right to walk to my car, or shall I carry you?'

Lisa shook her head. 'Just leave me here. I'll find my way . . . my way home.'

*'Non.'*

She leaned forward and her shoulders shook.

'Are you not feeling well? Please don't let the situation with Tasha worry you.' Julien couldn't help himself. He lifted his arm and put it around her shoulder.

'I have to. I shouldn't have lost my temper.'

'A saint would have lost their temper with that woman,' he said sympathetically.

'You don't understand. I should have ignored her. Until she pays me, I have no money and I have nowhere to go. I don't even have a car that I can sleep in.' Lisa turned her face into his shoulder again, and as he held her close, he realised that they could solve each other's problem.

Julien moved back slowly and gently held her shoulders. 'I think I have a solution that will suit us both very well.'

*** 

Heat suffused Lisa's cheeks as she stared into the dark eyes of the man who held her gently. She was sure that her blush was so deep he would feel it; maybe she could put it down to the flu and a temperature.

What on earth did he mean? Surely not what she had immediately thought, but all she could think of was the extremely sexy man she had watched on the screen. The characters he played were always jumping in and out of bed with women; beautiful women, she thought wryly. He wouldn't be thinking of her that way. Plain Lisa in her trackies and stained T-shirt.

But Julien's voice was soft and kind, and she couldn't look away as he lifted his hand and gently brushed his fingers on her uninjured cheek.

She closed her eyes and held her head stiff, forcing herself not to turn into his caress.

'We both have a need, and I believe that we can fulfill that need and be of use for each other. I will pay you and pay you well. You won't have to worry about money, and you won't have to worry about where you will live.'

*My God! Out of the frying pan into the fire,*

she thought.

Lisa let out a huff and folded her arms across her chest. Okay, so she'd made the wrong choice with Guy. No matter how desperate she was, and no matter how attractive Julien's offer was, she would not do that.

'I am not that sort of person,' she said stiffly.

'Shall I explain what I need before we go to my car?'

Her eyes widened, and she fought to stop her mouth dropping open.

*What he needed!*

Lisa sat straight and was about to protest again when Julien lowered his voice.

'I need someone to look after my child.'

*His child?*

As he explained his situation, mortification filled her. How could she have ever thought that his proposal was of a sexual nature? She had come within seconds of making an utter fool of herself for the second time in one night.

'Three weeks ago, I received a call from an attorney in San Francisco telling me that my daughter was about to be put on a plane and sent to me here in Australia.'

'You have a daughter?' she asked quietly. There'd been no mention of a wife or partner or

48

children when she had Googled him the other night. From all accounts on the sites she'd visited as she'd stalked him—heat flamed in her cheeks again—Julien Joubert had been born in Paris but had grown up on a farm near the artistic village of St Paul de Vence in Provence, because his actor father, Emmanuel Joubert, did not want his son to be raised in the glamour world of Paris. According to the gossip magazines, Julien had never been married but he always had a different beautiful woman on his arm in the photos.

Lisa had devoured the magazines last week, but there was no mention of a child.

'Apparently I do,' he said staring past her. His face was shadowed as he turned away from the streetlight and his expression was hard to read. 'I have an eight-year-old daughter who I collected from Brisbane three weeks ago. A daughter I had no idea existed until I received that call.'

'Where is she now?' Lisa asked.

'She is at home on my estate in the hinterland. The nanny who came over with her flew back to the States today. I drove her to Brisbane last night. My housekeeper agreed to stay over in the house with Sophie. Last night, *and* tonight so I could attend this stupid dinner. That is the reason I could not bow to the demands of Tasha.' Julien glanced at his watch. 'It is almost ten o'clock now. I am not going to go back to that circus in there.'

'Circus?'

'Yes. I hate all of the—what is the English word for all of the falseness that goes with the movie industry?'

'Superficiality? Sham?'

'Yes, both of those. I put up with it because I loved my craft and made my living from acting, but I had decided to take some time off. *Our Lost Love* is my last contracted movie for the time being. And now . . . now I have a daughter to care for. And I need someone to do that for me until this movie is wrapped up. Would you . . . would you be interested in the position? I think it would solve my problem and yours.'

Lisa was stunned; she shook her head, not knowing what to think or say. 'I know very little about children or how to look after them.' Her eyes widened as she stared at him, unable to believe what he had suggested. 'And you know nothing about me! I have no references. You have no idea of my suitability.' As she protested, she was wondering about the poor child, and trying to fathom what sort of mother would send her child to another country to a father she had never met. She *had* intended enrolling in a childcare course, but her reading about the course was the sum total of her experience with children.

Julien's low and sexy voice sent a strange feeling churning through her. 'I have watched you work. I have seen your kindness, and I have witnessed your integrity. I think you will be a perfect fit with Sophie. She is proving to be a delightful child, and all I need is for someone to be with her. Her care will be provided for by Mrs Whittington, my housekeeper. What I need is someone to take her out in the day, on picnics, for ice-creams and to the beach. With someone who will be kind to her and take responsibility for her safety. Someone she can laugh and play with. Someone who will show her how to have fun.' He shook his head slowly as he looked over her head. 'I don't even know if she can swim. I know very little about my daughter.'

Lisa's heart broke at the sadness in his voice, and her heart went out to the small child who was obviously now going to be in a shared custody arrangement.

'It is good that she is with you in time for Christmas,' she offered tentatively.

'It is.'

Lisa well knew how it felt to be unwanted as a child, and she knew what it could mean for the child's future, leading to making wrong choices and wrong decisions. She wondered how long the visit was for, and whether it was the beginning of shared custody. How the other half lived, she told herself. France, Australia, the United States, and nannies accompanying children halfway around the world. The lives of the rich and famous.

Julien reached for her hands and gripped them. 'Do I have to beg you, Lisa? I want the best for my daughter. I have advertised and interviewed strangers, but I did not find any of them suitable. Now that the nanny has returned to the States, I must have someone, or I will have to leave the movie. I do feel as though I know you well enough to trust you. I like you, and I know Sophie will too. She is surprisingly mature for her age.'

Lisa lifted her eyes as he turned her face to his, and the sympathy turned to longing. Julien Joubert was a kind and good man, and she had to push away the feelings that continued to ripple through her. Even though she was injured, little spasms of desire tugged at her and her dream was never far away.

Don't be foolish, she told herself. A man with those looks and that fame would never look at a plain Jane like her unless he had a need like the one he had articulated. If she accepted the position, it would help him out, she would get to spend some time in his company and could dream from afar before she moved on. It would get her some money, and she could buy her bus ticket back to Cairns.

And it would guide her in deciding if her choice of career and the childcare course was what she really wanted to do.

She stared at him and ignored the constant flutters in her lower belly and her shaking legs; those sorts of feelings had only ever got her into trouble before.

*Remember Guy.* Lisa shivered. She'd thought he was a decent person for a while, and then she had seen the creep behind the façade.

Julien was simply another man, a man with a problem and she would ignore those perfectly-shaped lips, the soulful eyes, the high cheekbones and the beautiful smile, and those gorgeous tumbling curls. She would forget her wonderful dreams.

Remember your past mistakes, she told herself sternly.

Okay, so he's got looks, money and fame. She would deal with that and ignore it.

His dark eyes bored into hers, and Lisa swallowed.

'So, what do you think? I don't want you to feel pressured, but I would like you to meet my daughter first, and then make your decision. If you decide not to take the position, I will pay you what Tasha owes you, and she can reimburse me.'

Lisa held his gaze and kept her voice calm

as she answered. 'I will meet your daughter, and I will accept the position. Perhaps we can discuss the terms tomorrow, and I can meet her then.'

'And where do you plan on sleeping tonight, *ma chère*?'

'I don't know.' She shrugged. 'Maybe the beach.'

Julien jumped to his feet and reached for her hand. 'You will come to my estate, and you can stay in the guesthouse. And yes, tomorrow we will discuss terms. We will retrieve your luggage from the apartment, and you and Sophie can spend the day in town getting to know one another while I work. I have to be on set for a short beach scene at eleven.' Lisa jumped as he slapped one hand to his forehead. 'But I am forgetting you are not well. Perhaps you should spend the day quietly with Sophie at the house.'

'I am feeling better, so I am sure I will be fine tomorrow. It will be good to have a decent night's sleep.'

Without worrying about displeasing Tasha and losing her job. Lisa smiled. That was done and dusted, and she was beginning to feel a lot better.

'Come. I have kept you out too long. My car is over here behind the hotel.'

Julien kept hold of her hand as they crossed the road. The street was still crowded with night-time revellers, and many curious looks were sent towards the man in the tuxedo and the girl in the tracksuit pants and stained shirt.

Lisa lifted her chin and smiled. It didn't matter what she looked like or what they thought.

Her idol, Julien Joubert, was holding her hand, and she had a new job. And she was sleeping in a guesthouse on an estate.

Maybe she should pinch herself to see if she was                                               awake.

# Chapter Six

Julien glanced across at Lisa a few times as the black Ferrari purred along the back roads between Sarnia Bay and his estate in the hinterland. She was quiet in the passenger seat beside him, but her head was turned to the window and her face was in the shadows. Deep relief had filled him when she had agreed to look after Sophie. What he couldn't get his head around was how this tiny waif of a woman had broken through his defences. He made a point of not getting involved with women; *certainement,* he would spend time with them, and wine and dine them, and go back to their apartment for the night, but he never let any of them get close to him. He would *not* repeat the decadent life his father had led, and the trail of children around the country. But Lisa had stayed in his mind since he had first noticed her in the ice cream shop; he had not been able to get her pretty face from his thoughts.

When Julien had moved away from Lisa, he had felt bereft. Her auburn hair had smelled sweet and she had been a perfect fit in his arms; he had wanted to keep holding her.

*Merde!* What had he been thinking? Lisa looked about sixteen-years-old, and she was in need of someone to help her out of a difficult situation and was certainly not someone for him to desire, no matter how beautiful she was. Julien gripped the steering wheel and, as he tried to push away the images of her beautiful face and her petite body, regret flooded though him.

*Another time, another place.* The circumstances were not right for him to be interested in this woman or to do anything about his attraction to her.

His father's choice of lifestyle had defined Julien's life and now he had his own guilt to cope with. He would *not* be like his father. Finding out that he had fathered a child and hadn't even known about Sophie, his daughter, had brought past tragedies and long submerged feelings to his mind.

*And what am I doing?*

Fighting an attraction to a young girl who had problems of her own. Disgust left a bitter taste in his mouth, and he made a vow that he would forget that Lisa was a beautiful woman. He would *not* be tempted.

He had so much to make up to Sophie, and as soon as this movie was wrapped up, he would devote his time to getting to know his little daughter and making sure she had a happy life.

He *must*. There was no other choice for him.

Easing back on the speed as the electric gates to his estate, *Villa Provence,* appeared ahead, Julien flicked a glance across at Lisa. She had put her head back on the leather headrest, and the faint moonlight defined her sleeping profile. Her lips were slightly parted, and long dark lashes fanned on her cheek as her chest rose and fell evenly as she slept.

His chest ached as though a punch from an assailant had landed in his belly. He took a deep breath as a long-forgotten feeling stirred only seconds after he had vowed that he would not let this woman get beneath his skin. He wanted to protect this vulnerable woman and keep her safe.

\*\*\*

A warm hand touched her shoulder and pulled Lisa from her dream. She smiled as she woke. Julien's lips had hovered over hers, and she had opened her mouth to welcome him. His bare skin had pressed against hers and she had waited for his kiss she wound her fingers through his long curls.

His breath brushed her lips. 'Lisa. Wake up.

We've arrived.'

Her eyes flew open, and she snapped her mouth shut. Julien's face was close to hers and his breath *had* brushed her lips, but he was simply trying to wake her up.

*It was another dream.*

Mortification flooded though her, and her face burned from a tell-tale blush.

*Oh my God, stop it.* At this rate, she would fight sleep when he was anywhere near her.

'I'm sorry,' she whispered.

'Sorry? Why would you be sorry?' His voice sent her nerve endings firing through her entire body, and one look into those gorgeous eyes had her doubting that she should take this job.

'I think I might have made a mistake.' Her voice was husky. 'I can't stay.' If she stayed here, she would end up making a fool of herself.

'Please wait before you decide. We haven't discussed the terms yet, but they will be very fair. Trust me, I am not like Tasha le Clair.'

*That's for sure.* Lisa stretched, and then covered her mouth with her hand as she yawned.

'I think I need to take you to your bed, and let you sleep.' With that, Julien opened his door and climbed out before coming around to the passenger side and opening her door. He held his hand out and his fingers were warm and firm as he helped her from the luxury car.

Memories of her dream and his warm lips sped through her.

'All right. I'll sleep on it.' Her voice was stronger, and her sore throat had almost gone. It was only a little bit scratchy, and as she stood, Lisa realised her headache was gone and her head was much clearer. She could breathe again.

They were parked outside a small brick cottage covered with sweet-smelling roses, and, as he led her to the bright yellow door, a security light clicked on and Lisa jumped. Looking up, she encountered a gentle smile as he looked down at her.

For a few seconds, she allowed her gaze to rove over Julien's face. His eyes were dark but the way he looked at her was unfamiliar. No man had ever looked at her like that before. His eyes held concern, and for a moment she thought she also caught a glimpse of something more.

Lisa shook her head. No, she was wrong. No man would look at *her* like that. She was still half-asleep, and back in her dream state. God forbid, she made more of a fool of herself.

Blinking, she tried to focus on the pretty cottage ahead, but found it impossible to look away from him.

Even in the semi-darkness, she could see

what a good-looking man Julien Joubert was. His cheekbones were high, eyes slightly tipped at the corners, flawless olive skin with full lips hinting at a passionate nature. She wondered how much of what she had seen in his movies was the real him. Another blush threatened; she had seen *a lot* of him in the movies, not to mention her dreams. There had been at least one love scene in each movie she'd watched, and the thought of him kissing her as he'd kissed those heroines sent a delicious shiver down her back.

She dropped her gaze to travel down to broad shoulders, down lower to narrow hips and strong thighs, hugged snugly by the fabric of his suit pants.

'Lisa?' Julien drew her name out, elongating the vowels so it sounded very French. It sounded so sexy a shiver ran down her spine.

'Yes?' When she looked up, the concern in Julien's eyes had been replaced by something else; something that told her that he was fully aware of what she was thinking. Another tremble ran down her spine and continued down her legs as his gaze swept over her body. His eyes flared with interest as they returned to her face.

Cold reality hit.

*Wake up to yourself.*

This man—the movie star—not the real man

standing in front of her and still holding her hand, did things to her. She turned and focused on the door ahead, and ignored the unfamiliar desire tugging at her.

It was the movie star, not the real Julien who was making her feel that way. A good night's sleep and the cold light of day would bring her back to reality. Away from soft moonlight, sweet-smelling roses and shadowed profiles hinting at secret kisses and whispered words of desire.

*Oh God, Lisa. Wake up!*

She waited for him to answer but he continued to look at her without speaking.

'It's a very bright door,' she said to break the tension. Because there *was* still tension. The way Julien was looking at her was no longer in her imagination, although she had no idea why.

Finally, he reached past her and opened the door. Clearing his throat, he stepped back to let her enter ahead of him. 'I bought this estate last year, and the builders have renovated and replicated my home in Provence. It soothes me and is a restful place to be when I am in Australia.'

She walked in ahead of him, and the room was flooded with light as Julien flicked the switch behind her. 'You plan to spend more time here after the movie is finished?'

As she looked around the beautiful room, he

came and stood beside her. 'I do. Especially now. Sophie doesn't speak any French yet, so I think it will be easier for her if we live here for a while and she can go to a school where she knows the language. I am pleased that I have recreated my Provence home here in the Sarnia hills. It will be familiar to her when I take her to visit France.' He looked pleased. 'There is an orange orchard too. Just like home.'

'What about your movies?'

'I had planned to take a break anyway.'

'Your fans won't like that very much.' Lisa hid a smile. She would have to make sure she downloaded copies of all of his movies onto her iPad.

'I would prefer to give Sophie a stable life instead of dragging her all over the world and having her sat by a procession of different carers. I want her to know that I care about her, and that I will look after her.' The fierceness in his voice surprised Lisa.

'That is admirable. She is a very lucky little girl to have a father who cares so much.' Her voice held bitterness. She had never known her father, and her mother had died when she was a small child.

'I care for her very much already.'

*Already?*

'I will leave you to sleep, and you can meet

her in the morning.' Julien stood straight and lifted his hand and then pulled it back. His voice was distant, and there was no more talk of family or empathy.

'The bed is made up and there are fresh towels and toiletries in the bathroom.' He pointed to a door on the other side of the living room. 'And there is coffee, and snacks, in the kitchenette. Please make yourself at home. I will come down in the morning and drive you up to the house for breakfast.'

'Drive me?'

'Yes, the house is another two miles into the estate. If you need anything through the night, there is a phone here that will connect to the main house by dialling nine.'

'Thank you, I am sure I will be fine. I am feeling much better.'

Again Julien lifted his hand, and then put it down before he turned to the door. 'Goodnight, Lisa. And thank you. I will see you in the morning at nine.'

She shook her head and took a step towards him. His eyes were hooded as she reached out to touch his arm. The slippery white silk of his long-sleeved shirt was soft beneath her fingers. 'No, it is me who must thank you for rescuing me from Tasha. If you hadn't stepped in, I'd probably be sleeping on the beach.'

Julien moved away from her touch, and for a second, Lisa wondered if she had overstepped the mark. But as his hands lifted to her shoulders and he pulled her close to him, she closed her eyes. His lips brushed her forehead, and his words were quiet. 'I will see you in the morning, *ma chère*. Sweet dreams.'

When she opened her eyes, Julien was gone, and the door closed quietly behind him. Lisa stood there as the car started up outside and she watched through the lead-panelled window until the taillights disappeared up a long drive.

It was a long time before she went in search of the bedroom.

# Chapter Seven

Lisa woke the next morning to dappled sunlight filtering through pretty lace curtains. She snuggled deeper into the feather pillow and soft mattress, opening her eyes slowly trying to remember where she was.

*At the guest house at Julien Joubert's estate!*

She felt like pinching herself; it was hard to believe she was here. All her doubts of the night before seemed to have evaporated with the dawn of a new day. A day where she no longer had to worry about pleasing Tasha le Clair's every whim. She was here at Julien Joubert's estate—*pinch me*—and she had another job.

Her night had been filled with the most delicious dreams. She stretched languorously, her bare skin against the smooth cool sheets reminding her of her dreams. Of course, Julien had played the starring role. Her imagination had replayed scenes from his movies, and she had taken the lead female role. Her cheeks warmed as the dream floated away, as dreams do when you wake up.

It didn't hurt a girl to dream. Especially if it made her feel like this. She had never experienced feelings like this before; never had this all-consuming need for one man gripped her so strongly.

Last night, after having a quick wash in the amazing marble bathroom, she had stepped out of her clothes, fallen into bed, and dropped immediately into a deep sleep. The virus that had made her feel so bad must have been a twenty-four-hour bug; she was almost recovered this morning. Climbing out of bed, Lisa padded across to the window and lifted the curtain. The sun was high in the sky and she wondered what time it was. A lush rainforest, separated from the house by a narrow, cleared paddock where two horses grazed, sat nestled beneath a mountain. Small colourful birds flitted in and out of the trees and she smiled, looking forward to the day.

This was paradise.

Life was good for the first time in months. This was what she had expected when she had set off from Cairns for a three-month holiday. Happy days when she felt content.

Lisa stepped from the bedroom into the large living room they had entered last night, and her eyes widened when she looked at the ornate clock on the wall. It was five minutes to nine; she hadn't slept this late since she had started out on the trip with Guy. Hurrying back into the bedroom, she grabbed two towels from the wrought iron stand beside the door and cast a baleful glance at her clothes on the chair, wishing she had something nice to put on today. Having to go up to the big house and meet Sophie dressed in them took some of the gloss from the day ahead. When—if—Tasha paid her, she would ask Julien if she could go to town and buy some new clothes. There was very little in the apartment of her previous employer. Most of her clothes had been in the van when Guy had taken off. She left the towel for her hair on the back of the sofa in the living room. She would go out into the sunshine and dry it when she was dressed.

The water from the huge shower head was hot and strong, and Lisa stayed under there longer than she meant to. As she washed her hair, the sweet fragrance of the shampoo and the conditioner lightened her spirits even more, and for the first time in days, she began to believe that things were going to improve for her. She would agree to take the job looking after Sophie until Julien's movie was finished—she assumed that would be another month or so, but that depended on how long the set shut down for over Christmas. She knew Gaz was keen to wrap the project up; Lisa had overheard him assuring Tasha of that when the older woman had complained about the Australian heat.

'You'll be home to your English snow as quick as a flash, love,' he'd said, winking at Lisa behind Tasha's back. So hopefully the shooting would continue for another month and she would have a month of looking after Sophie. That would set her up well enough to go back to Cairns and find a job before she started the course.

Lisa turned the taps off, quickly dried herself, and then bending forward, she wrapped the damp towel in a turban around her head. She wouldn't have time to go out into the sun now so her hair was going to have to be finger-combed when she was dressed. Even though the bathroom was well equipped with products, there was no brush or comb in sight and hers were still in Tasha's apartment.

Opening the bathroom door Lisa stepped into the living room.

Before she could take one step, her eyes locked with those of the man who had filled her dreams all night.

Julien slowly crossed the room towards her. Her mouth dried and her heart raced as he reached for the towel on the back of the sofa, his muscles rippling beneath his snug T-shirt. He held the towel up and embarrassment flooded through her as she stepped into it.

\*\*\*

'Wait here, Sophie. I'll collect Lisa, and you can meet her.' Julien had told Sophie about Lisa this morning when they'd had an early breakfast together. 'I won't be long.'

'Yes, Daddy.'

He put the four car windows down to let fresh air in, before he hurried down the short path to the guest house. Sophie's acceptance of him as her father had been instant; considerably faster than the knowledge that he had fathered a child had been accepted by him.

But he had no doubt that she was his child. As well as her being the image of him, the attorney had also provided sufficient proof for him not to doubt the truth of her paternity, and he had been in a relationship with Corinne Abbott, the girl's mother, nine years ago, before his career had taken off.

The mystery was why Corinne had never contacted him. He would have taken immediate responsibility and provided for Sophie if she had told him she was pregnant. Julien glanced back at the car. Sophie was sitting quietly and smiled at him when he looked over.

Whatever Corinne's reasons had been, she

had done a fine job of raising their child.

Julien smiled back before he knocked on the front door. When there was no response, he knocked again, and when all was quiet, he frowned, pulled out the key and opened the door. Hurrying across the living room, he headed for the bedroom to check that Lisa was all right. Before he was halfway across, the bathroom door opened, and she stepped into the living room.

His eyes widened as she stood in front of him, her alabaster skin translucent in the morning sunshine. Her skin was flawless, and the apricot tips of her breasts were the only colour against her perfect white skin. He quickly forced his gaze upwards and spotted a clean towel on the back of the sofa. He grabbed it and opened it wide, keeping his eyes on hers, and away from her bare skin. She stepped forward and that glorious body disappeared behind the white towelling. He wrapped it around her; his fingers ached to touch her, but common sense prevailed.

'Thank you.' Her voice was low and husky, but she wouldn't meet his eyes.

'My pleasure, *ma chère*.'

'I'll go and get dressed.'

'Daddy!' Julien turned as a plaintive voice called from the door. 'I'm sorry I got out of the car, but it was hot.'

'That's all right, Sophie. We won't be long now.' When he turned back to the living room, Lisa had disappeared into the bedroom and the door was closed.

He walked across to the door and tapped before speaking loudly. 'Lisa, we have been to town and your bag with your belongings is in the car. I'll bring it in, and we'll wait outside for you.'

A muffled 'thank you,' came through the closed door.

He took Sophie's hand and they walked outside together. The ease with which his daughter had accepted her situation, and how she trusted him astounded Julien every time he looked at the little girl. 'Wait here, and after I take Lisa's bag inside, we will go and say good morning to the horses.' Her happy squeal had the horses lifting their heads and ambling over to the fence.

'Yes, Daddy.'

Julien shook his head as he retrieved Lisa's bag from the back of the car. Sophie had been a perfect child so far. Not a cross word, no shyness, and she seemed happy to fit in with anything he asked. Even when he had met her at Brisbane airport with the nanny who had accompanied her across the Pacific Ocean, his daughter had known who he was and that she was going to live with him from now on; she had accepted him without question.

He tapped on the door and slid the bag inside before walking over to the car and taking Sophie's hand again. 'Come on and meet our new horses,' he said. Her little hand slipped into his, and the emotion that rose from within finally dispelled the hunger that had consumed him since Lisa had stepped naked from the bathroom.

*Maybe hiring her had been a mistake. Maybe he should have hired one of the several he had interviewed.*

And then he remembered the cutting words that Tasha had lashed him with when he had asked for Lisa's things while Sophie waited in the foyer, chatting to the concierge.

An unfamiliar young woman had opened the door to him. Tasha had obviously already replaced Lisa with a new PA, and the young girl scuttled to her command and soon had Lisa's clothes packed and handed over to him.

Tasha had refused to hand over Lisa's pay cheque.

'I meant every word that I said, Julien. She was in breach of *her* contract. I will see your acting career is over and done with. How dare you take the word of a slut like that over mine! I will ruin you.'

He kept his voice even and his words quiet. 'And if you do, Tasha, this movie will flop, and you won't be in demand again. Think about that.' He turned to go and then hesitated. 'Not that that would worry me unduly. I can't say it's been a pleasure. Oh, and did I tell you? This was my last movie.'

Tasha stamped her foot, obviously unable to think of a suitably scathing reply.

Julien turned to the young girl who stood wide-eyed by the doorway. 'Do you have a contract? You think carefully about how much you need this job.'

The scream of the aging star rang down the hall to the elevator. Five minutes later as he and Sophie walked to his sports salon, Julien found it hard not to smile when he saw Tasha's new PA exit the apartment building carrying a suitcase.

He was very pleased that Lisa was now in his employ.

# Chapter Eight

Lisa's hands were still shaking as she pulled her only dress over her head. She had to get over this juvenile attraction to Julien; she was acting like a starstruck teenager. His nonchalance when she'd stepped out of the bathroom without her towel had convinced her of that. It had been a huge thing for her when he'd walked in on her—God, even thinking about it sent heat zinging through her again—but he'd been so casual about it, it had obviously been no big deal for him.

She had to grow up. And fast. But that was easier said than done. It had been very thoughtful of Julien to get her bag; he must have gone into town early. Composing herself, she quickly brushed her wet hair and scooped it up and secured it with a tortoiseshell clip. She looked around the room. The bathroom was tidy, and she'd made the bed, unsure of where she would be sleeping tonight.

Picking up her small case, Lisa took a deep breath and headed outside. She blinked and pulled her sunglasses over her face; the summer sun was bright as well as hot on her shoulders. It wouldn't take long for her fair skin to burn in this heat.

Julien was standing by the fence with a small girl. He was crouched beside her and the child had her hand on his shoulder as she looked at him. Lisa hesitated and then walked over to the fence.

'But why don't they have names, Daddy?' Her voice was soft and sweet, her American accent strong.

'I think you should give them their names. What do you think?'

'Really? I can?'

He nodded. 'You can.'

Julien looked up over the little girl's head and smiled at Lisa. His smile warmed her. 'Lisa, this is Sophie. My . . . daughter.' His voice held a strange note, a note that was hard to distinguish, and she wondered why he hesitated. 'Sophie, this is my friend, Lisa.'

The little girl turned around and clapped her hands. 'Oh boy. That is swell. You're going to look after me, and Daddy said we are going to have lots of fun. And you can help me think of names for the horses now.'

Lisa crouched down and smiled as Sophie held out her hand. She drew in her breath as she looked into a pretty little face that was almost identical to Julien's. 'I sure hope we do, Sophie. We can explore Sarnia Bay together. I do know where there is an excellent ice-cream shop. Do you like ice-cream? It's my favourite food.'

Julien nodded. 'Lisa used to work there, so she knows all the flavours, I'd say.'

'How did you know that?' Lisa looked at him curiously.

'I saw you there last week. You served Sophie. We both said how pretty you were, didn't we, Sophie?'

'We did. And I had the double strawberry and caramel waffle cone. Do you remember, Lisa?'

'I'm sorry. It was always so busy I didn't take much notice of the customers.' A thrill ran through her.

*Julien had said he thought she was pretty.*
\*\*\*

The afternoon after Sophie arrived, he'd first noticed Lisa at the ice cream shop. Julien had sent Sophie into the shop to choose and pay for her ice-cream. He'd kept a close eye on her as she'd ordered and handed over the money and waited for the change. Pride had filled him as he'd watched the little girl's confidence and maturity.

She'd turned and run out to him, and he'd stopped looking at the pretty girl with the flawless skin. 'Look, I did it all by myself. The money in Australia is pretty.'

Julien had crouched down beside her as she licked the double cone. 'You are a very clever little girl.'

'I am not a little girl.' The American accent was pronounced. 'I am eight-years-old.'

'*Très bien*, you are a very clever big girl.'

Sophie's eyes shimmered with tears for the first time since she had arrived. 'That's what Mommy said. I'm a big girl and I have to be brave.'

Not worrying about the risk of strawberry ice cream on his silk shirt, Julien had pulled her close. 'You are a clever and brave big girl, *mon petit chou.*'

'What does that mean in proper words?' Sophie asked, the tears forgotten.

'It means you are my little cabbage.'

'Ew, that's gross. I hate cabbage.'

Julien had laughed with her, but as he stared over her head, he'd wondered how the hell he was going to cope with the situation. The movie took second place behind caring for Sophie, but the watertight contract meant that he had to complete the remaining scenes.

If Lisa agreed to take the position now she'd

met Sophie, he would be able to fulfill his commitments. His only concern was how skittish Lisa seemed around him. Walking in on her as she'd come out of the bathroom had added to the tension between them, although he had tried very hard to hide his reaction. The thoughts that had gone through his head had been R-rated. His fingers had itched to draw her close and caress that beautiful skin, but he had played it cool.

He stood and nodded towards the car. 'I think it's time we showed Lisa our house, Sophie.'

'Oh yes, come on, Lisa, you can sit in the back with me.' Sophie ran off to the car, and Julien turned to Lisa. Her cheeks were flushed.

'I'm sorry I didn't ask you how you were feeling today.' He lifted his hand and placed it on her forehead. She trembled beneath his touch. 'You feel cool, but your colour looks as though you still have the fever.'

'I'm fine,' she said quietly.

'Excellent. We will talk before it is time for me to leave. We can talk about what I would expect from you. Then you can decide if you would prefer to stay at the house today or if you and Sophie come to town with me. Do you have your driver's licence?'

She nodded. 'I do, but I can't drive your car.'

'Why not?''

'It's a Ferrari! I can't drive that. I'd hate to damage it.'

Julien couldn't help himself. He reached over and took her hand. 'It's a car, and it is at your disposal. If it bothers you, we will see about getting you a smaller sedan while you are here. I want you to be able to take Sophie around. Today, you can drive back here if I am held up, and I will hire a driver to bring me back when we finish.'

He smiled when her eyes widened.

'We'll see.' Her smile was tentative, and a surge of protectiveness washed over him. He didn't know what it was, but there was a vulnerability in Lisa that made him want to fold her in his arms and keep her safe.

That feeling was at odds with his other desire to take her to his bed.

Julien opened the passenger door. 'Sophie, Lisa can ride in the front with me. You will have her to yourself for most of the day. It is my turn to talk to her now.'

Sophie happily climbed into the back and Julien waited until Lisa was in the front seat before going around and putting her case in the back.

As they drove up the winding drive that led to the main house, she kept her face turned away and looked out the window.

But Julien did notice her hands clenched tightly in her lap.

# Chapter Nine

'I sure love that you do my jigsaws with me.' Sophie clapped her hands together and leaned forward and picked up one of the pieces in the box. 'Look, I found his nose!'

Lisa smiled as she watched the little girl carefully put the piece of the reindeer's nose in the correct place. 'You are very good at them.'

'Oh, I love Christmas,' Sophie squealed. 'Do you, Lisa?'

*Not this year*, Lisa thought, but she nodded and tried to look excited. 'It will be fun to be with you.'

'You can help me hang my stocking on the tree. You should see the huge tree my Daddy put up for me. It's in the other living room upstairs. Closer to the chimney so Santa can find it more easily. Just as well I'm in Australia. We won't need a fire. It was snowing when I left my Grandma's house.'

This morning, an excited Sophie had

showed Lisa her bedroom, and the one next door where Lisa would sleep, and then she'd met Mrs Smith, the housekeeper. It had been a mutual decision to stay at the house while Julien went back to Sarnia Bay to the movie set. Part of Lisa's motivation was that she wouldn't be expected to drive the car back to the estate if Julien was held up. Sophie had clapped her hands—she had done that a lot today—and said there was so much to show Lisa, she'd rather stay home at Villa Provence too.

'But tomorrow, I want to go to the shops so I can buy Christmas presents.'

Julien and Lisa had sat over coffee while Sophie had her morning tea outside in the play area, and as Julien had spoken to her, Lisa had tried to react calmly and rationally, as though he wasn't the sexiest man on the planet.

Her survival tactic would be to spend as little time in his company as possible. He would be on the set for many hours, and when he was home, he would be with Sophie and she could disappear.

'Those conditions are very fair,' she said after he had outlined the expectations and the salary she would be paid. 'In fact, too fair. The salary is very high.' Lisa concentrated on keeping her hand steady as she lifted the fine porcelain coffee mug to her lips.

'When it comes to my daughter, nothing is

too much.' Julien held her gaze and that ever-present tremble ran down her back again. When he came home today, she would stay in her room and let him spend time with his daughter.

Lisa nodded. 'Thank you. I appreciate it. And don't you worry about her today. We will have fun. She is a lovely little girl, and I'm looking forward to spending the day with her.'

Julien put his cup down and stood. 'Excellent. Tomorrow, we will drive to the Gold Coast and go to the Pacific Fair shopping centre that I have heard is a good place to shop. We can all do our Christmas shopping.'

A pang of sadness lodged beneath Lisa's breastbone. This was her first Christmas without Nan and she really had no shopping to do. Although she would buy something for Sophie.

*And Julien,* a persistent voice nagged in her head.

'*Très bien.*' He touched her arm lightly as she stood up beside him. 'We will have a good day. Mrs Smith is going to prepare a cold luncheon for us on Christmas Eve. Perhaps we will think of some table decorations, and you can help me shop? *Que penses-tu?* I mean, do you think that would be all right?'

Lisa cleared her throat. 'Yes, I can help you and Sophie.' It would only be a few hours in his company.

Julien had left and Sophie had requested her help with finishing the jigsaw puzzle, and then when that was over, she had decided to show Lisa the gardens.

If only she could stay away from Julien—and the shakiness that came along with his presence—she could last the month or so out.

\*\*\*

It was late afternoon by the time Julien drove into the estate. He pressed the remote and closed the electric gates behind the Ferrari and let out a relieved sigh that he was home. Tasha had been impossible to work with and even Gaz had lost his temper. As he locked the car and walked from the garage at the back of the house, laughter reached him from the orange orchard halfway up the hill. He smiled as Sophie's giggle filled the still early evening air.

'I give up, Lisa. And then it's my turn to hide this time.'

'Okay, I'm coming.' Lisa's laugh joined Sophie's and a sense of wellbeing dispelled Julien's unsettled mood.

He walked up the hill and into the orchard, the smell of blossoms in the air was overpowering and even though it was late in the day, he could hear the buzzing of the bees as they moved among the creamy blossoms.

'Daddy!' Sophie's squeal pierced the air. 'You can play now. We've had the best fun all day. But Lisa won hide and seek. I had to give up.'

Before he could reply, there was a rustling of leaves and a scream from above him. As he looked up, Sophie squealed again from the next row of trees. 'There she is!'

Lisa's scream joined Sophie's; there was a loud crack, and as he looked up the branch Lisa was lying on began to tip. Her arms flailed and then Julien caught a glimpse of an expanse of long bare legs before he realised she was falling.

Feeling like one of the stunt people in the movie crew, he held his arms wide and took a step backwards as Lisa fell towards him. He bore the brunt of her fall, and before he could react, they were lying on the ground beneath the tree in a tangle of arms and legs. He was on his back, and Lisa's body was full length along his.

'Oh my God, I'm so sorry. Are you all right?' Her green eyes were only centimetres away from his, and he could feel her panting breath on his lips. Julien smiled, lifted his arms and looped them around her waist, holding her firm against him. She was lying full-length on top of him. He hadn't changed after his outdoor scene today and he was wearing a pair of board shorts and a T-shirt. Her bare legs were warm against his and his hands brushed against bare skin where her crop top had ridden up above the briefest pair of shorts he had ever seen. Julien lifted his arms and took hold of Lisa's shoulders and repositioned her slightly to one side to avoid embarrassing her.

'I've never been better,' he said huskily. He lifted his hand to hold her head gently and Lisa didn't resist as he slowly pulled her closer, inch by inch, until the warm skin of her neck was against his mouth. Her soft skin smelled of flowers as he slid his lips up along the side of her neck until his lips reached her cheek. An almost imperceptible moan of pleasure whispered against his skin as Lisa's mouth opened as he claimed her lips. To his pleasure, he—

'Daddy! Did you find Lisa. I couldn't see her!'

Lisa drew back and stiffened in his hold as Sophie came running through the trees towards them.

'You won! Can we have another game and Daddy can play this time?'

Lisa moved against him, attempting to get up, and Julien's body responded accordingly.

'Please let me up,' she said softly.

'Of course.'

Sophie stood there with her hands on her

hips as Lisa scrambled to her feet. 'Can we play again? With you this time, Daddy.'

'I didn't realise how late it was,' Lisa said, tugging at her top to cover her bare midriff.

His eyes followed the movement of her fingers as the luscious expanse of pale skin disappeared. 'Spoilsport,' he said softly.

'Sophie, it's time to go back to the house. Maybe, your dad can play hide and seek with you another afternoon.' Lisa walked towards the gate.

Sophie grabbed for his hand and Julien smiled.

'Come on, Daddy, come and see what we did this afternoon. It was so special.'

As Lisa walked ahead of them, Julien tried to keep his attention off the delectable figure in front of them. Already he was regretting kissing Lisa; it had been a foolish thing to do. He should not have given into temptation.

He would not do it again.

# Chapter Ten

Even though she hadn't really wanted to have dinner in the main dining room, Lisa couldn't help smiling as she sat at the table with Julien and Sophie. Dinner was a happy meal, and Sophie giggled as she recounted the story of Lisa falling on top of her daddy to Mrs Smith as the housekeeper served the simple meal of grilled chicken and vegetables. Mrs Smith was a pleasant woman who had welcomed Lisa with a wide smile. When Lisa had suggested eating dinner in the kitchen—to avoid Julien—the housekeeper had shaken her head.

'Don't be silly. We don't stand on ceremony here. The American nanny girl ate with Mr Joubert and Sophie, poor little mite. It's good for Sophie to have some young company with her, and besides, if you eat in the kitchen, it makes more work for me.'

Lisa gave in, although she did help carry the meals into the formal dining room. The table was a twelve-seater setting, but they all sat at one end.

Julien seemed to be in a good mood; when Sophie had finished recounting the story of the tree—for the third time—with a mischievous glint in his eye, he told Lisa about Tasha falling over at the water's edge during filming today.

'Oh no, the poor old thing. I hope she was all right.'

Julien's grin widened. 'She loves me again because I rescued her and carried her up to the director's chair, and she took great pleasure in sitting in the chair and leaving the cushion soaking wet.'

'Oh dear, she can be so awful.'

'She—'

'Lisa?' Sophie interrupted them. 'You haven't eaten all of your vegetables.'

Lisa looked down as the little girl drew attention to her half-finished meal. Nan had taught Lisa her manners and she'd placed her cutlery in the middle of the plate without thinking. 'I've had enough to eat. It was lovely, but I'm not very hungry tonight.'

Julien's hooded gaze held her eyes as though he knew exactly what she was hungry for. Lisa dropped her eyes.

'You have to eat all of your vegetables.' The little girl's voice shook.

'Sophie.' Julien reached over and took his

90

daughter's hand. 'It is all well. Lisa is a guest, and she said she has finished her meal.'

'No!' The pitch of her voice increased. 'Mommy told me that I had to eat all of my vegetables and I would stay well. Lisa, you have to eat yours too.' The little girl's lip quivered as she stared at Lisa. 'I want you to be well too.'

'It's okay. I feel a little bit hungry again. And besides—' Lisa leaned across to Sophie and whispered— 'I did see some jelly and ice-cream in the kitchen, so I guess I had better eat all my dinner if I want dessert.' The depth of the little girl's distress was obviously genuine, and Lisa knew she wasn't putting on a tantrum for the sake of it.

Sophie's face lightened as Lisa cut into a Brussel sprout and put it into her mouth and managed to chew without gagging. At the same time, she was trying to stay cool, as Julien's eyes seemed to be on her each time she glanced across at him. As soon as dessert was over, she was going to put Sophie to bed, and disappear into her room. She had bathed her before dinner, and Sophie was in her PJs already. There was a widescreen television in the cosy sitting room on the balcony side of Lisa's room, but Lisa knew one thing. She would not be watching a Julien Joubert movie tonight. After lying so close to him this afternoon, she was in enough trouble. Never had she been so aware of a man, and as hard as it was to believe, she knew from the way that his hooded gaze stayed on her that he was in the same mind frame.

What would it matter if she slept with him? If he really did want to.

It would be something to remember after she had left and gone back to Cairns. A night in the bed of a famous movie star.

*Her favourite movie star—could she do it?*

*Oh, yes, her body screamed out.*

*No! Her sensible side chimed in.*

'Good girl, Lisa!'

Lisa jumped and switched her attention to Sophie, and then she looked down at her plate, surprised to see that in her preoccupation, she had eaten all the vegetables on her plate.

'Daddy, may I leave the table and tell Mrs Smith we are ready for our ice-cream now?'

Julien nodded. 'You may.'

The little girl slipped off the chair and carefully lifted her plate and cutlery from the table and took them with her.

Julien waited until she had disappeared into the kitchen and Lisa jumped as his hand touched her wrist. 'Thank you.'

She smiled at him. 'You owe me. I loathe Brussel sprouts.'

'I noticed. You did well. Thank you for

calming Sophie. It's been a difficult time for her.'

'When does she go back to America?'

Julien's brow lowered in a frown and his dark eyes were intense. 'Why would she?'

'To go back to her mother?'

His voice was quiet as his fingers slid along her wrist and he gripped her hand. Her nerve endings kicked in and warmth travelled up her arm.

'Corinne died two months ago. That's why my daughter has come to me. And that's what Sophie was talking about when she wanted you to eat your vegetables and stay well.'

# Chapter Eleven

'That's my favourite story, Lisa. Now, we have to have just one more.'

Lisa forced a smile as Sophie snuggled down into her bed. It was hard knowing that Sophie's mother had died; her thoughts were whirling. How had she not known that Sophie was here to stay?

'Why do I get the feeling I'm being conned into reading more stories than you usually have?' She reached over and smoothed a hand over Sophie's dark hair, hair the same colour as her father's.

When Julien had left the room after he'd been in to kiss Sophie goodnight, he'd nodded at Lisa. 'Come down to the living room when you are finished here, please.'

'Just this one more story and then I'll go to sleep, I promise. Plee . . .eee. . .ease, Lisa? This one is a special one from my mommy.'

*How could she resist that sweet little smile?* Lisa took the book that Sophie held out. It was called *The Invisible String*.

As she read the words to Sophie, about the connection of love to people you have lost, she found it hard not to cry, but Sophie was looking at her wide-eyed and nodding as Lisa turned the pages.

When she turned the last page and closed the book, Lisa swallowed. 'That was a lovely story. Now it's time for you to go to sleep so we can have another fun day tomorrow. I think your Daddy is taking us shopping.'

'Cool!' Sophie sat up in bed. 'Lisa? Can I have a hug?'

'Of course you can.'

As Lisa pulled the small girl in close for a goodnight hug, she just heard her soft whisper. 'Before my mom went away, she said that one day I would get a new mommy. She said I had to trust Daddy because he would choose a princess for himself one day. Do you think you would like to be my new mommy, Lisa? I think you'd be very good. Maybe have a think about it.'

Lisa's breath caught. How did you answer a question like that?

Before she could think of an answer, Sophie continued. 'I didn't know my daddy before I got here, and he is just like the prince that Mommy told me he was. He had to go away to his movie kingdom and make his treasure, so I hadn't even seen him. Not ever. Now I've seen my daddy in front of the cameras and all, I know what it is. It's like my Disney channel on TV. He is like a prince, don't you think, and you know the best thing?' The little girl drew a big breath.

'What's that, sweetie?'

'Before Mommy said goodbye to me, she said he would love me forever.'

'I know he will.' Lisa smoothed Sophie's hair back again and waited for her to lie down. 'And yes, he is a prince,' she said softly. 'Your daddy is a real prince.'

'So will you think about what I asked?' Sophie pulled the blanket up to her chin and gave Lisa an angelic smile before she closed her eyes.

Lisa's throat ached as she left the room, and as soon as the door was closed, tears spilled over. Julien had taken on a daughter he'd never seen, he'd been kind to that bitch, Tasha, and he'd helped Lisa when she needed help.

He was a good man, a kind and caring man, and that was a big part of her attraction to him.

An attraction she must fight. Poor little Sophie, already looking for a new mother.

'Lisa?'

She looked up, blinking the tears from her eyes as the door on the other side of Sophie's closed quietly. Julien stood in the hall.

'She's asleep. She goes off quickly.'

'Sophie's had a good day with you. You've kept her busy, and happy.'

'She's a sweet little girl.'

'She is. Come down to the living room, and I'll make us a coffee—or maybe a drink—while I tell you about the past few weeks.'

'Okay. I'll just freshen up. A drink would be nice.'

'White wine?'

'Yes, please.' After that emotional bedtime experience with Sophie and waiting to hear what Julien had to say, Lisa knew a drink would relax her and help her sleep. No longer were her thoughts focused on what had passed between them this afternoon; all she could think of was a sad little girl looking for a new mother.

But only one small glass. She couldn't risk relaxing her guard too much. Being downstairs alone with Julien was fraught with danger, but a quiver of anticipation ran down Lisa's spine despite her best intentions.

\*\*\*

'Make yourself comfortable, please. The story I have to tell you is one of love.' Julien worried about how ill-at-ease Lisa looked sitting opposite him on the single sofa. Her back was straight, and her hands were clenched in her lap.

'Thank you. I'm fine,' she said when he passed her the glass of crisp, cold wine. Her eyes were red-rimmed, and her cheeks were flushed, and he wondered how much Sophie had told her already. Lifting his glass to his lips, he was surprised when his hand shook. Julien cleared his throat and began the story.

'Late last month, the same week the movie crew arrived in Sarnia Bay, I received the call from the attorney I told you about. I didn't go into detail last night because I was worried about you after your accident, and then, as unlikely as it sounds, the fact that I hadn't told you about Corinne slipped my mind.'

'What happened to her?' Lisa's eyes were sad.

'Let me start at the beginning.' He leaned forward and put his wine glass on the coffee table separating them. 'I met Corinne when I first went to LA. She worked in the food van on the movie set. It was my first movie.'

'*All That We Have*,' Lisa said quietly.

He smiled. 'You know my movies?'

Her cheeks heated and she nodded. 'Only since I started working with Tasha. I like the stories you tell. Very much.'

'Thank you. I choose the scripts that I read very carefully. I like my movies to convey a message. That's why it's taken me a long time to become successful.'

'I've seen all your movies in the past week, and I can see that.'

'Thank you. That means a lot to me that you have noticed. And that you took the time to watch them. Anyway, as I told you, I hate the sham and artifice of the movie world. It was so bad those first months I spent in LA, I almost went back to France. But then one day when I was between scenes, I had a longer lunch break, and I met Corinne. In all the falseness of Hollywood, she was like a breath of fresh air. She sat with me and we talked for a couple of hours.'

Lisa nodded and as she kept her eyes on him, Julien looked away. Looking at her filled him with thoughts that weren't appropriate as he told her the story. 'Corinne was so different from all the would-be starlets who were after a role and would do anything to get one. And I mean *anything*. Corinne was her own person. She had no interest in being in the movies and she was building up her natural food business. We had a wonderful month together.'

'What happened?'

'I was the male lead in *All That We Have*, and I had to go on location in Mexico. I begged her to come with me, but every time I would ask her, she smiled and said it was my rising star that I had to follow, and she was content where she was.' Julien swallowed. It was still hard to talk about those days. The guilt that had come slamming in when he had heard that he had fathered a child with Corinne had been almost impossible to deal with. He was no better than his father. Julien had four half-siblings and he had sworn not to follow in his father's footsteps, and yet he had found out that he had a child he had known nothing about. Sophie, who he already loved, and who he vowed to care for until he took his last breath. Knowing that Corinne had died alone and had made such detailed plans for their daughter had broken his heart.

'Julien?' He looked up as a warm hand held his tightly. Lisa had moved from her chair and was on the sofa beside him. He blinked as Lisa's face moved closer to his. 'It's all right, you don't have to tell me. Now that I know that Sophie doesn't have a mother, I'll try to provide what she needs.'

Julien shook his head, trying to compose himself. He lifted his arm and brought it around Lisa's shoulders. 'Thank you, but I want to tell you the rest. So, you understand my daughter as best you can. I still can't believe how mature and composed she is. I worry that it's been too soon, and she is coping too well. *Alors*, she has lost her mother, travelled halfway around the world to live with a father who didn't even know she existed.

'You have all the time in the world to help her grieve and heal. She's suffering quietly in her own way,' Lisa said. 'How long has it been?'

'Just under a month. But as soon as I met Sophie, there was a bond. Corinne had made sure I was a part of her life without me knowing about her. She knew all about me, and she said she had been looking forward to meeting me one day. It's hard to believe, but I loved her from the moment I saw her.'

'And she already cares about you,' Lisa reassured him. 'That is obvious.'

'I have Corinne to thank for that. I left her in LA.' Julien stared ahead. 'When I called her from Mexico, she told me she had moved on, and I believed her. She was a free spirit. In the letter she left with the attorney, she said once she found out she was pregnant with Sophie, she decided to go it alone, as she knew my star was rising, and she didn't want to interfere with my dream. She kept saying that and she convinced me. If I'd known she was pregnant, I would have gone straight back and married her.' He lowered his head and looked at the floor, but his voice was bitter. 'I didn't contact her again. My star had risen.'

Lisa's words were soft, and her hand was still holding his. 'You can't blame yourself. Corinne had made her choice. And she may not have married you, but it sounds like she had prepared Sophie very well for the future.'

'Yes, she was a free spirit, but kind and caring. I have no doubt that she was the best mother to our child.' He shook his head, unable to comprehend how Sophie was handling this so well. *He* wasn't handling it.

'May I ask what happened?'

'It was a blood disease. Swift and relentless, but still she had enough time to write to me, see the attorney and prepare Sophie.' Julien looked down at Lisa's small white hand holding his firmly. 'It's my job now to get Sophie through the next few months as the reality of Corinne's death hits home. I have withdrawn from my future contracts. She is my priority now.'

'That's an excellent plan.' Lisa's thumb smoothed the back of his hand. 'By the time I leave, you should have a routine started, and Sophie will be settled into school.'

'Please don't talk about leaving.' He lifted his head and pinned her with his gaze. 'It's very early, but I know the more that I talk to you, and the more I see you with Sophie, that I want you to stay.'

'At the most it could only be two months. I've enrolled in a childcare course in Cairns.'

'When does this course start?'

'In March.'

'That is very soon.'

'Maybe I could change my plans. Let me give it some thought.'

He was pleased to see her lips tilt in a smile.

'Perhaps I could stay for a *little* longer.'

'It would be good for her to get to know you. It appears that Sophie knows me well already, and I know she trusts me from whatever Corinne has told her.'

'It's a very sad situation, but I am happy to help out while I can.'

'Thank you, Lisa. I think we were meant to meet. Even if it was through Tasha. As Corinne used to say, the universe is looking out for us.' Julien couldn't help himself. He leaned across and brushed his lips across her forehead. 'I do appreciate you being here,' he said softly. 'Now I want to know a little bit more about you. Tell me how you came to Sarnia Bay.'

# Chapter Twelve

The bright colours of Christmas and the carols playing through the huge shopping centre made for a happy mood. Tomorrow was Christmas Eve, and Julien was not required on set today so he'd driven them up to Pacific Fair to buy Christmas presents.

Lisa was the happiest she'd been for a long time. She clutched her purse tightly, still not used to having money again. Not only had Julien managed to get Tasha to pay her for the two weeks she'd worked for her, but he had also insisted on giving her an advance on her salary. When she had filled him in on her background last night, and told him how Guy had ripped her off, he had been angry, but his mood had lightened when she'd tried to pay him back the money she owed him for the cold and flu tablets.

'I left the rest of the change from your hundred with Tasha.'

Julien grinned. 'And that's where it has remained. She is a devious woman. Don't worry, it won't break me.' He kneeled in front of Sophie. 'I'm going to go and get the things on Mrs Smith's list while you two ladies wander around the shops. There is a food court in here somewhere. I'll meet you there in an hour.'

Lisa smiled. 'I think I see someone who doesn't like shopping very much. What do you think, Sophie?'

Julien's eyes held hers as he grinned up at her. 'No, you see someone who wants to have time to buy some presents too. What would you like for Christmas, Lisa?'

She shook her head. 'You don't have to buy me anything.' The way his gaze pinned her made her legs shake.

*In the middle of a shopping centre for goodness' sake!*

The one thing she really wanted, she couldn't have. She *wouldn't* have.

The smile he sent her way was secretive, and she knew he was going to buy her something. Lisa and Sophie headed off, and she realised that if Julien was buying presents, she should probably get something for him. She could get in the Christmas spirit too.

'So, Sophie, what are we going to buy for

your Daddy for Christmas?'

The little girl giggled. 'I know exactly what he would like. Mommy left me a list.'

'Your mommy sounds like she was a very organised person. Tell me what was on the list.'

Five shops later, and laden with many parcels, Lisa and Sophie headed for the food court. There was a crowd milling outside the coffee shop where Julien had texted them to meet him, and Lisa wondered what was going on. As they drew closer, she could see him surrounded by a group of women. Two were each hanging onto an arm, and he looked as though he wanted to escape.

'Oh no. I think your Daddy has been recognised.' Spying an empty table, Lisa put their parcels down and indicated a chair for Sophie to sit down. 'Wait here, sweetie. I'll go and rescue him.'

Once Sophie was settled, Lisa strode through the tables and reached the group. 'Julien, darling. We're back.' She bit back a smile at the relief on his face and walked over and stood there until the woman on his left moved away. Standing on her tiptoes, Lisa reached up and brushed her lips across his mouth. 'Sorry ladies, I'm going to have to take this man of mine away from you.'

Julien took her hand and smiled as the women drifted away. '*Mon Dieu,* I was very pleased to see you walking towards me.' His grin became cheekier. 'I was even more pleased when you kissed me.'

'I thought it would make them realise you had someone with you, and that I wasn't just another fan.'

His voice was intense as they walked back to the table where Sophie was waiting. 'You are already a lot more than that, *ma chère*. But that is something that we will explore when you are ready.'

Lisa's legs went to jelly as he held her gaze. There was something in his eyes. How could she feel like this in the middle of a crowd in a shopping centre? All she could think about was the feel of Julien's warm lips beneath hers as she had brushed them ever so briefly. She was going to have to make sure that she never found herself alone with him.

She trusted him; it was herself that she didn't trust.

His hand was warm on her back as he guided her to the table and pulled a chair out. The warmth lingered and made its way further down. Maybe the present she'd bought for herself wouldn't go to waste. Sophie had been occupied in the store when Lisa had spotted it, and she hadn't been able to resist.

*Just in case. Dream on, girl.*

'Have you shopped enough?' he asked as

they looked at the menu on the table.

'Yes, we have finished.' Lisa kept her eyes down, aware of the curious looks being sent their way. She could just imagine the comments. 'Look that's Julien Joubert! Who on earth is that plain woman with him?'

Her mood plummeted and confusion filled her. Was she reading him totally the wrong way?

*I am!*

Julien's interest in her was purely because of what she could do for Sophie, and how it would help him out. He probably had Christmas functions, and parties to go to tomorrow. He was being polite; she would babysit Sophie to free up his day.

Lisa stared down at the menu, her appetite gone.

Sophie was engrossed in the screen of a small game that they had bought in the department store where Lisa had bought Julien's gift—a silk shirt.

The next few days were going to be hard to get through. She'd be pleased when Christmas was over, and he was back on set.

*** 

Julien saw the instant when Lisa was overtaken by self-doubt. Her body language changed, her shoulders slumped, her expression closed, and it was as though she tried to become invisible. His heart went out to her; she was so fragile and vulnerable he wanted to protect her. He would love to get his hands on that *goujat* who'd dumped her and taken her money.

'Daddy, can I have a ride on the merry-go-round?' Sophie's attention had been caught by the small fair in the centre of the food court.

'Of course.' He turned to Lisa. 'Come with is, we'll sit over there on the bench seat and watch Sophie.'

Lisa nodded, but her eyes were distant.

Julien sat on the seat close beside her. Her eyes widened when he reached over and took her hand. 'Thank you for rescuing me before. I was very grateful to see you coming.' He lowered his voice. 'I was most grateful for the kiss you gave me.'

'I shouldn't have done that.'

He reached over and gently took her chin between his fingers. 'Look at me, Lisa.'

When she obliged and slowly lifted her beautiful green eyes to meet his, it was hard not to take her in his arms and kiss her right there and then.

'This might not be the right place to tell you how I am feeling, a crowded shopping centre is not very romantic.'

Her eyes widened and her lips parted

slightly. His attention dropped to the tip of her tongue as she licked her lower lip. Such a simple movement, but one that had an instant effect on him.

'Romantic? What do you mean, how you feel?' she whispered.

'What you are doing to me. I can't take my eyes off you.' He lifted her hand to his lips and brushed a kiss over her knuckles.

'Me? But I am not beautiful.'

'Oh yes, you are, Lisa. With your beautiful skin, your glorious hair, and Cleopatra eyes, you are a very beautiful woman.'

'Me?'

'Yes, you, *ma chère.* It's so very hard for me not to reach out and touch you when I am near you.'

'You've only known me a few days.'

'Trust me. I know what I feel.' He turned her hand over and kissed the centre of her palm. Her soft gasp told him what he'd been hoping for 'I would hope that we can explore this at a more appropriate time, *que dis-tu?'*

'I don't know what you are saying when you use French words.' Her colour heightened. 'But they do sound pretty.'

'I was asking you what you thought about that.' He let go of her hand. 'We will leave it for now. Here comes Sophie.'

# Chapter Thirteen

Julien was called to the set early on Christmas Eve while Sophie and Lisa were having their breakfast. Lisa had been a bundle of nerves all night as she'd relived the words that he'd said to her in the middle of the busy shopping centre. She wasn't sure what she was supposed to do, what she was supposed to say, or what he expected from her. She lay in the bedroom next to Sophie's all night wondering if Julien would come to her. If he did, she would welcome him.

*But no*. Of course, he didn't knock on her door. Why would he? Plain Jane, Tasha had called her.

Lisa finally went to sleep just before dawn, and it seemed only minutes later that Sophie came running in and jumped on the bed. 'Santa comes tonight!'

All Lisa could think was how grateful she was that Julien hadn't been in her bed when his daughter had come running in. It wouldn't be the right thing to do. It would give Sophie more ideas about her being a mother candidate!

Without Julien there, the day dragged by. Mrs Smith invited Sophie into the kitchen after lunch to help her make gingerbread men, and Lisa yawned as she decided what to do.

'Mrs Smith just said we can make a gingerbread house too, to decorate the table tomorrow. Do you want to come and help too, Lisa?' Sophie was jumping around with excitement and Lisa wondered how she would ever get her to sleep tonight.

'I think I'll go and have a rest in the hammock by the pool,' she said. 'Call me when you're finished. Or if you need me. We have a big day tomorrow, Sophie. I'd say you might wake up very early.'

'What time will Santa come in Australia?' Sophie's mouth opened in a wide O. 'Do you think he'll know I'm here? Or will he go to our house in America?'

'Of course, he'll know,' Lisa reassured her.

'Come on, Sophie, we have a lot of work to do if you want to get this gingerbread house made. And then we have to set the table for Christmas lunch tomorrow.' Mrs Smith sent Lisa a sympathetic look. 'You do look tired, love. Go and have a rest. I'll look after Sophie for the afternoon. Remember, I won't be here all day tomorrow.'

## 

Lisa changed into her bikini and had a quick swim in the pool before she lay in the hammock to dry off. It was the first time she'd had time to herself since before Guy had left and she revelled in the freedom. She lay back and looked at the bright blue sky through the lacy green canopy of palm fronds above her. As the hammock rocked slowly in the breeze, her eyelids were heavy. Of course, her daydreams sent her straight to Julien, and she lay there rocking, letting her imagination take flight. If she couldn't have the real thing, she could indulge in a daydream.

A smile lifted her lips as she let the hammock swing.

Something crawling on her shoulder stirred Lisa a while later. She opened her eyes and looked around. The sun was low in the sky; it was mid-afternoon. She was surprised by how long she'd slept. Another tickle on her shoulder had her looking behind her and her eyes met a pair of dark sexy eyes, full of teasing . . . and something else. Lisa mouth opened slightly as she looked into Julien's eyes and she watched as his gaze lowered.

'May I kiss you, Lisa?'

She nodded and waited. 'Sophie?' she

whispered.

'Sophie and Mrs Smith have gone to Ballina to buy some essential ingredients for a gingerbread house. I passed them as I came up the driveway five minutes ago. They won't be back for at least two hours."

'Oh,' Lisa said. For a moment she blinked, wondering if she was still dreaming. She lifted her eyes to his face and her gaze lingered on beautiful lips that were coming closer to hers.

She arched to meet him, and there was no need for words. Her stomach fluttered as his lips closed over hers, and his hand gently caressed her cheek. With his free hand he took both of her hands and lifted them above her head and the hammock rocked gently.

'Am I dreaming?' she whispered.

Julien lifted his head and held her eyes with his. 'No, *ma chère*, you are not dreaming. Perhaps it would be better if we adjourned to my room. That is, if I am not going too fast for you. Please tell me that you are happy for me to kiss you?'

Lisa reached down and brushed her fingers along the ridge that was obvious in his fitted board shorts. 'I will be very happy if you keep kissing me.' She blocked the thought of not being beautiful for him. If Julien wanted her, that would be enough. Even just once.

He stood, lifted her from the hammock, and carried her through the door and up the steps to his suite. Gently lowering her to the floor, he flicked the lock over on his door and turned to her. She shivered as he cupped his hand around the back of her neck and pulled her to him. His other hand was on the wall beside her.

He placed a lingering kiss on her lips and slid his mouth down her cheek and along the nape of her neck.

Her fingers crept up and she grabbed the bottom of his T-shirt. 'Kiss me again, please.' Lisa was surprised by her brashness, but it came naturally from a place deep within. She wanted this man with every inch of her being.

\*\*\*

Julien leaned back and looked at Lisa's beautiful face. Her lips were parted softly, and the tip of her tongue ran across her bottom lip.

He rested his forehead against hers. 'I have fought this feeling and I swore I would not touch you, but God help me, you have bewitched me. You are so beautiful.'

Her eyes widened and she frowned at him. 'There is no need to pretend. I am not beautiful.'

He shook his head and ran his fingers through her glorious auburn hair. 'How can you think that? If I have to spend the rest of my life convincing you, you are beautiful, so be it.'

'With words like that you are a very skilled lover.'

'With a beautiful woman like you in my bed I hope I can give you pleasure.'

He took Lisa's hand and led her to his bed. Julien drew a breath as he looked down at her lying on the dark blue sheets. 'You are more than beautiful, *ma chere*, you are perfection.'

It was a long time before wither of them spoke again.

# Epilogue
*Christmas morning*

Lisa woke up in her own bed just on dawn as there was a quiet tap on her door.

'Lisa, Santa Claus has been. Quickly, come downstairs.' Sophie's excited words were followed by a deeper voice.

'Hurry up, Lisa. We're not going to open anything until you come down. Are you awake?'

'I am.' Her voice was husky, and her smile was wide. She was sure she had smiled all night. By the time, Mrs Smith and Sophie had arrived home, she and Julien had been sitting on the lower balcony watching the sunset over the mountains. His eyes had barely left her, and each time he rose, his hand would caress her shoulder or her hair.

The gingerbread house was soon finished, Mrs Smith gave explicit instructions for heating up the Christmas dinner, and wished them all a Happy

Christmas before she left for two days.

They had sent Sophie to bed early, and when she was sound asleep, Julien had taken Lisa to her bed to say goodnight.

That had taken until midnight. Four more wonderful hours with him. She stretched and the cool sheets caressed her skin. Before Julien had left her room last night, they had talked and talked, and she began to understand the man he was.

'I am not a star, Lisa. That does not define me. I am a man trying to make a difference. Now that I have Sophie, I will give away my profession for a few years. I may go back to it, I may not. Tell me about you, tell me what you want.'

He had listened as she spoke of her difficult childhood, and her loneliness, and her grief when her grandmother had passed.

'I was planning to enrol in that childcare course so I can make a difference in children's lives in some way.'

Julien rolled over and held her close. 'Would you consider giving us a trial and staying here, and making a difference in one little girl's life?' His finger had touched her lips. 'Don't answer me now. 'Think about it.'

'I will,' she had breathed before his lips had descended on hers again.

Jumping out of bed, she had a quick wash

and slipped on the beautiful cream silk gown she had treated herself to for Christmas. She was surprised to see Julien and Sophie waiting for her in the hall.

'Merry Christmas, Lisa!' Sophie's arms went around her waist and Lisa dropped a kiss on that dark hair.

'Merry Christmas to you, darling Sophie. Let's go down and see what Santa has brought for you.'

'Not yet.' With a cheeky grin, Sophie pointed to the mistletoe that had somehow appeared above Lisa's bedroom door. 'You have to kiss Daddy Merry Christmas, first. That's what mistletoe is for.'

Lisa turned to Julien and smiled. 'You're right. That's what it is for.'

Julien opened his arms and she stepped into them as his lips lowered to take hers in a lingering kiss.

'Happy Christmas, Julien. I have two things to tell you.'

He held her at arm's length and that gorgeous smile made her toes curl. 'Two things?'

'My answer is yes. I would love to be Sophie's nanny.'

Sophie squealed and Julien kissed her again. 'I will thank you properly tonight,' he whispered so that only she could hear. 'Now what is this second thing?'

Lisa knew her eyes were bright with happiness as she stared up at her employer, her lover; the man she knew would have a part in her future.

'No matter what you say, Julien, you will always be my Christmas star.'

THE END

# Christmas with the Boss

## Annie Seaton

# Dedication

*This book is dedicated to my whole family.*
*Christmas is for family time!*

# Acknowledgments

*A special thank you to my wonderful editor*

*and dear friend, Susanne Bellamy.*

# Chapter One

*Christmas Eve*

Jilly Henderson joined the end of the queue at the only gas station in the quiet little beachside town of Sandy Heads. She folded her arms and settled in for a long wait; it was Christmas Eve and it appeared everyone was stocking up on their last-minute snacks before the shops shut for Christmas Day. Glancing down, she smiled as a pair of large, tanned, sandy, *and* bare feet in front caught her attention. She straightened and lifted her eyes a fraction, enjoying the sight of tightly-muscled calves above those bare feet. Tilting her chin higher, her leisurely perusal continued up tanned skin lightly brushed with blond hair, up to firm thighs that disappeared into a pair of board shorts moulding one of the most perfect male butts she had ever seen. Down south, her feminine bits that had been dormant for *way* too long gave a little jiggle.

"Always check out the size of their feet, girls.

Big feet, big—"

"Sharyn!" The giggles that had gone around the office contrasted with the corporate black suits and classy chignons of the executive assistants on the tenth floor of the bank building in George Street. Between the bouts of frantic activity that happened on the trading floor twenty-four hours a day, Jilly spent most of her work day shaking her head at Shaz's antics and hilarious advice.

Blonde-haired and elegant Shaz always managed to come up with a dry comment to break the tense atmosphere of the trading floor. The one about checking out the size of a guy's feet before accepting a date had the girls howling with laughter.

'Because you know what that means, ladies!'

When the boss had lifted his head and frowned through the glass wall of his office, they all quickly put their heads down and focused on the coloured numbers on their screens.

Now Jilly stared down at the feet of the guy in front of her. Not that he'd be interested in her, but this guy had *big* feet.

*Huge* feet. Sharyn would say that was a yes. Jilly stifled a grin and let out a soft sigh; the pretty young things chattering away in front of him were keeping his attention on the front of the queue. Surfer boy wouldn't be interested in a tired and frazzled city girl.

She hadn't been on a date for over a year, so she hadn't had a chance to put Sharyn's test into practice. *And* those girly quivers below were few and far between these days, so that little tremble low in her belly did put a smile on her face. Memories were nice.

Jilly needed no one; she was here at the beach to have a total break. Work had been hectic leading up to the festive season, and with many nights of Christmas functions, drinks and farewells she was feeling burned out.

Five days of bliss, alone, no work and no one to bother her beckoned.

Mr. Big Feet took a step forward as the queue moved and Jilly shuffled along closer to the counter. Her gaze lingered on that tight butt, clad in snug-fitting boardshorts, before she lifted her eyes to feast on a golden tanned back. No harm in looking.

*Oh, my.* She swallowed.

Broad shoulders lightly dappled with freckles had a sprinkling of sand stuck to the smooth skin. Small grains were embedded in the sexy hollow at the top of his shoulder. It made her think of lazy afternoons lying on the sand. Jilly literally had to curl her fingers to stop herself from reaching up and brushing the sand away. Maybe the surf god wouldn't be impressed if a tired and stressed-looking woman with dark circles beneath her eyes ran her fingers over that glorious back. To distract herself, she turned away and looked out at the cars in the fuel bay, trying to pick which one was his.

*Of course.* A beat up 1970s Kombi van with two surfboards secured to the roof racks was at the front of the line. Jilly nodded to herself; that would be surfer boy's car. How good would it be to jump in with him and head up the coast to Byron Bay? That was sure to be his destination—a mecca for surf gods.

*A girl could dream.*

Another step forward in the queue and she turned her gaze back to him, unable to resist one last look.

His curly brown hair was sun-bleached on top, and the thick, springy curls just brushed his shoulders. Even his neck was strong and tanned.

She fanned herself as her wicked imagination kicked into overdrive and tilted her face up toward the frigid air blowing from the vents in the high ceiling. Even though artificial, the air was blessedly cool. A welcome relief after the strong smell of petrol that had pervaded the hot bay as she'd filled her car. It was just on dark, but Jilly was sure the mercury was still registering over thirty degrees outside.

Summer down under. *Bliss.*

Not to mention her internal temperature was sizzling as the erotic fantasy filled her mind. What a sad life she must lead to be fantasizing in a gas station! This short holiday was *way* overdue.

It had been a long, long drive from Sydney. The sooner she found the beach cottage and fell into bed the better. Exhaling with a tired sigh, Jilly shuffled forward another step as the queue moved at a snail pace.

"No, the party's at the surf club *tonight*."

Jilly tilted her head to the side, looking past the surf god's broad shoulders towards the girl who was chatting to the cashier. Mary, the cashier—Jilly could just see her name tag—reached for the milk that the customer had placed on the counter. The register beeped as she scanned the plastic container.

"Tonight? I thought the party at the surf club was on New Year's Eve?" The pretty young girl in a red sarong pushed her hair back from her face as she lifted the rest of her groceries onto the counter. Her voice rose shrilly.

Mary chewed gum as she shook her head—no rush here. The dozen or so customers in the queue ahead of Jilly almost let out a collective sigh as they jiggled their feet, tapped hands on thighs and looked at their watches. Even the surf god's shoulders tensed a little, sending another pleasant little ripple through her belly.

*Country service.*

But Jilly liked it; people-watching was fun, even if she was tired. In Sydney, you were lucky to get a hello in any store. Now Mary, the slow-moving cashier, leaned on one elbow and imparted the correct information about this party to anyone who was interested. "No, it's tonight. Starts in a couple of hours."

"Really?" The girl in the red sarong leaned forward. "Are you sure?"

"Yes, it's at the surf club *tonight*. The New Year's Eve *party* is at the pub on the river."

"Well, I'm not missing either of them. Have you seen the talent in town this week?" Jilly resisted a nod as the 'talent' in front of her stretched to his toes and the muscles in his calves flexed.

"All the local surfers are home for Christmas and the parties will be hot!" The young girl pushed her hair back from her face as she turned apologetically to the person in the queue behind her. "Sorry, I remembered I just have to grab some party supplies. Won't take a minute." She flicked a glance back to the cashier and her mouth split into a grin. "Just as well I've already been to the bottle shop."

"Got your priorities right there, love." Mary, the cashier's, voice held a tinge of sarcasm.

"Oh, for God's sake." Impatience filled Jilly as she watched the girl head for the fridges lining the back wall. The next customer in line stepped up to the other register but Mary waved him away.

"Sorry, love. The other cashier is on a tea break. You'll have to wait." She flicked open a magazine on the counter and began to read, ignoring the cross mutterings of the waiting customers.

Jilly closed her mouth as another yawn threatened.

*What was one more delay?* Her day had been fraught with them since she'd hit that first red traffic light in Manly this morning. Anyone would think she was having a bad luck day. Black cats, ladders, broken mirrors, shoes on tables—her dad had been a sucker for superstitions and Jilly knew them all. She swallowed as she pushed that thought away; her grief was on hold until she was ready to deal with it.

The entire trip up the coast from Sydney had been a nightmare from start to finish. Heavy traffic had choked the M1 as what had seemed like the entire population of the city, headed for the beaches of the north for the annual break between Christmas Eve and the New Year. Dad had always told her not to leave Sydney on Christmas Eve, but Jilly had been so keen to get away from the city after the

129

funeral, she'd decided to put up with the traffic.

But it had turned into a ten-hour trip, instead of the five it should have taken. Despite the six-lane freeway, a broken-down truck near the Gosford interchange had added two hours to her trip. Finally, after crawling through slow bumper-to-bumper traffic, she'd called into a small town just south of her destination to stock up on groceries for her eight-day break. Once she got to the beach cottage, she had no intention of getting back in her car until she left after the New Year.

Keen to travel the last short leg of the trip, she'd hurried out to her small sedan with her few grocery bags and groaned. An old, battered utility had her car parked in. Jilly had sat on the grass verge in the hot sun, fuming for half an hour until an elderly couple pushed their laden trolley across the car park. The words that she'd had ready to blast the car's owner died away as she watched the old man hold his wife's hand and place her carefully in the front seat, before he slowly unpacked the trolley into the back of the ute. Jilly couldn't help herself. She pushed to her feet and helped him unload.

"Thank you, my dear." He went around to the front of the car and came back with a small parcel and pressed it into her hands. "Merry Christmas. One of Ethel's plum puddings for you."

Tears welled into Jilly's eyes and she ran the

back of her hand over her face; emotion had clogged her throat for the whole trip, but she wasn't going to give in. "Merry Christmas to you and your wife too."

He drove away sedately; still oblivious that he had blocked in Jilly's car. With a sigh, she'd pulled out and hit the highway again.

Smothering a yawn with the back of her hand, she rocked on her feet as she waited and looked over to the brightly-coloured products on the shelves along the wall. Everything to tempt the sweet tooth she tried her best not to indulge.

*Bad move.* On the back seat of her car were three bags filled with salad makings, and fruit. Shaz and Elise, the perpetual dieters at work had taught her good habits; there was no Christmas cheer for her apart from Ethel's plum pudding. Jilly smiled as she stepped away from the queue. She was at the rear, so if she was quick, she wouldn't lose her place.

Picking up a basket she headed to the fridge and opened the door. A minute later her basket was filled with a carton of custard to go with the plum pudding, five small bottles of full-cream strawberry-flavoured milk—she wouldn't tell the girls at work—two family-size chocolate bars and two trashy magazines. Jilly stepped between the shelves and threw in two bags of potato chips for

131

good measure on her way back to the queue. No one had joined it and she got to stand behind the surf god again.

The girl in the sarong was still loading her basket. It was Christmas; Jilly had to dig deep to find some Christmas spirit. Finally, the girl came back to the counter, paid for her party goodies and the queue began to move more quickly. There were now only seven customers ahead of Jilly and she covered another yawn with one hand.

A second cashier appeared behind the counter and the queue moved again. Jilly reached down to pick up her basket as surfer boy reached the head of the queue and paid for his fuel. Bending down, she reached for her basket as he turned to pass her. She glanced his way as she straightened. Did the face match the perfect body?

*Oh. My. God.*

Jilly froze and forced her open mouth to close. If you *could* freeze when prickles of heat scorched your skin.

"Miss Henderson." Her boss, the senior group executive and chair of the Executive Committee of the SBA bank stopped walking and flashed a smile at her. Perfect white teeth, the same sexy grin that she'd admired every day for the past six months. She'd tried to ignore her good-looking boss since he'd arrived at the bank mid-year. But now, the tailored business suit had been replaced with a bare chest and those low slung boardshorts, and the fantasy of the last ten minutes now left her gasping for composure. Her mouth dried as she stared at the V of dark blond hair that disappeared into the shorts below his navel. The muscles on his chest were as ripped as the rest of him. Who could ever have known what that business suit hid?

"Mr. Smythe-Phillips," she finally managed to croak out.

"Feeling peckish, are you, Miss Henderson?"

"What?" Jilly lifted her eyes from his bare stomach to meet a pair of eyes crinkled with laughter.

*Sprung perving at his chest. How embarrassing.*

His grin widened as he pointed to her plastic basket.

Relief flooded through her; he was talking about the food. Jilly swallowed and forced the huskiness from her voice. "Ah yes, um . . . er . . . um . . . some holiday supplies," she stuttered and stumbled over her words like a teenage girl with a crush.

Thank God, he hadn't noticed her when she'd been salivating over him in the queue. There was no way she could have sustained a conversation with him for any length of time with him half-naked in

133

front of her; she would have died of embarrassment. It was bad enough to be caught out in a pair of skimpy shorts, and a tight-fitting T-shirt. At least he was on his way out and she didn't have to make social conversation for long.

"See you back at the office next week. Have a good Christmas . . .Jilly." His voice was as deep and sexy as ever and her name rolled off his tongue. She'd never noticed what a sexy voice he had before.

Jilly nodded mutely.

He really was just too gorgeous; for six months she'd managed to hide how she'd dreamed about Dominic Smythe-Phillips. And that was when he was in a business suit. Now he'd morphed into a tanned surfing god, she was a goner. How the hell she'd ever sit across the board table without thinking of that bare chest when she went back to work . . .

Jilly stared after Dominic as he opened the door of the silver Audi TT Roadster that was parked behind the Kombi van. Wrong again.

Little warm tingles were having a fun time down in the now ex-dormant zone.

"Stop perving and hurry up, love. You're holding up the queue." Mary's drawl was amused as her gaze followed Jilly's. "Bit of a looker, is our Dom, isn't he?"

Jilly closed her mouth and turned to the waiting cashier.

*Our* Dom?

# Chapter Two

Dominic Smythe-Phillips turned his sleek sports sedan onto the dirt road that skirted the beach. He deliberately looked away from the first cottage and turned his attention towards the beach. Purple shadows cast by the setting sun hovered on the glassy water. The last rays caught the slow-moving swell as it pushed to shore, breaking as a bridal veil of foam on the wet sand. Even though the waves were small, there was a nice right-hand break on the point, just catching the last glimmers of light from the sun as it sank below the Great Dividing Range to the west of Sandy Heads, the small town where he'd learned to surf.

*Should be great for a surf in the morning.*

But surfing tomorrow wasn't at the forefront of his thoughts. The skimpy shorts and the figure-hugging tank top were very different to the attire of Miss Henderson of the corporate suits and high heels. If it hadn't been for the glorious copper-toned hair that cascaded down her back, Dominic probably wouldn't even have recognised the woman behind him as his executive assistant. The lush image imprinted on his mind since Jilly Henderson had gaped up at him in the gas station wouldn't go away. The same woman who had caught his eye the day he had been appointed as chief of the Group Executive at the biggest bank in Sydney. There'd been muttered comments about special treatment when she'd been promoted to his executive assistant, but it hadn't taken much to dispel the gossip. He was used to it; corporate banking was a bitchy and cutthroat environment. He recognised talent and hard work; good looks were a bonus.

He wondered idly where she was heading and then focused on the surf. They hadn't shared their Christmas plans; the office was too busy for personal conversations. And he much preferred to keep work businesslike without the social chitchat that went on in the lunchroom.

Kept the rumours at bay. Although he did wonder what Jilly Henderson had been up to lately. Usually one to stay late at her desk, in the last month she'd been leaving as soon as trading ceased for the day, and then she'd had a few days off last week. Personal time, she'd said with no further explanation. She got her work done, so it was none of his business.

Dominic shrugged as he turned to the ocean.

And she did her work very well; she had a keen eye for the stock market and on more than one occasion Jilly Henderson had directed his attention to recent trends before he'd noticed them.

*Forget work.* He was here for a break.

If the swell stayed small, he'd get his knee board out and wax it ready for the morning. Didn't matter that it would be Christmas Day; he had no family left in town.

*Nice legs, though.*

It had probably been stupid to come up here in his rare time off from work, but it was as good a time as any to try to put his memories to rest. Long overdue.

*And cute freckles too.*

He'd hit the sack as soon as he'd waxed his board. Pleasant tiredness tugged at Dominic's muscles; he'd been in the water all day on his large board. He'd hit the surf early again tomorrow; his knee board should still be in the small wooden shed attached to the old building at the back of the cottage.

The familiar and long-loved smell of salt and seaweed met Dominic as he climbed out of the Audi. He grabbed the carton of beer he'd picked up from the pub and walked through the long grass to the old cottage. He'd have to pull out Pa's old mower while he was staying here. He stood on the front steps and looked back down the road. It had been a long time since he and Derro had walked together down that road on their way to high school . . . and to the surf. When they'd been teenagers without a worry in the world.

And it had been almost as long since he'd last been down to the other cottage: his grandparents' cottage. Not since Derro's funeral. Dominic pushed open the door and the fresh smell of the ocean was replaced by the musty smell of an old house that had been locked up for a long time.

*Pretty eyes too.*

He grinned again as green cat-like eyes fixed on his stomach flashed into his head. The prim Miss Henderson had been checking him out. He'd never noticed those cute freckles on her nose either. Maybe he'd break his own rule and ask Jilly Henderson out for dinner when they got back to the city.

# Chapter Three

Jilly threw her junk food purchases onto the back seat next to the healthy groceries. Shaking her head, she peered up the road, but the silver Audi was out of sight.

*Who would ever a thunk it?* Shaz would say with a giggle. Fancy Mr. Iceberg being up here on the north coast. Shaz had soon branded the new boss with his nickname, when it became quite clear he was not up for socializing . . . or flirting. It was only last week that the girls had been speculating about where the sexy Dominic would spend Christmas. Jilly had been quiet, and her colleagues had been sympathetic about her losing Dad.

London, Paris, or skiing at Aspen had all been mooted for the boss. Slumming it north of Sydney hadn't rated a mention. What had the cashier meant by "our Dom"? Anyway, it would be fun to recount her experience of checking him out in the gas station to the girls in the office; they'd get a laugh out of that. She hadn't contributed much to the usual hilarity in the lunch room these past few months.

Then again, maybe she wouldn't tell them just how delectable he looked in his boardshorts. She'd file that little picture away for the meetings where Mr. Iceberg sat business-like in his dark suits, barely cracking a smile as he concentrated on profit margins and stock movements. Anyway, that was work; this week was for much needed relaxation and regaining her emotional strength after nursing Dad in his final days. It was time to forget about him. Jilly grinned—it was hard to compare the new Dominic with the one she was familiar with.

She turned on the GPS as she drove back onto the main road and headed for the beach. Several wrong turns and a good hour later, she finally turned onto the sandy road that led to the address on the receipt shoved into her bag. The GPS had kept telling her to turn right—into the ocean.

The sun had set, and darkness was falling quickly. She hoped the key to the rental was where it was supposed to be; the guy on the phone had been vague and hard to understand with his soft muffled voice. She frowned as a long, deserted road loomed ahead of her. Tall trees encroached on both sides and there was no sign of any houses. She stopped and pulled the receipt out: yep, that was it—Swimming Creek Road. Jilly knew she was finally on the right road; she'd seen the sign when she had ignored the robotic voice of the navigation system, followed her instincts, and turned off the esplanade.

She frowned; no luxury cottage fitting the description of Beachside Vista was anywhere to be seen. She'd checked out the holiday rental online when she'd received an email advertising a vacancy over the holiday break; the photographs had displayed the interior of a spacious cottage decorated in a retro style across from the beach. Not that she really needed spacious for the few days she'd be here. Her car moved slowly along the narrow road and the beachside she-oaks formed a dark canopy above her, and she stared ahead trying to see in the murky light.

The sandy road narrowed even more, and the frequent potholes got deeper. Jilly shivered as a feeling of gloom pervaded the early evening. Suddenly a house appeared ahead of her to the left and she almost overshot the driveway. She hit the brakes and the car pulled to a stop. An old wooden sign hung crookedly from a post in the long grass at the side of the narrow road proclaiming she had arrived at Beachside Vista.

"Oh, no." A groan escaped her lips.

An old weatherboard cottage loomed out of the darkness as she stepped from the car. She squinted in the dim light. The paint was peeling, and loose guttering hung in a jagged, rusty spiral, scraping noisily against the side of the house. The wind had picked up and another shiver ran down her back as it keened eerily through the trees, the breaking ocean providing a mournful background.

All it needed was a storm to make it totally spooky.

*Crack!* Jilly jumped a foot. A clap of booming thunder instantly followed the flash of lightning that lit the sky almost as though she had summoned it.

Okay, she'd wanted privacy but maybe not quite *this* much isolation. The knee-length grass brushed against her bare legs and she turned back to the car for the small torch she kept in the glove box. Small creatures rustled in the long grass and she stepped quickly back to the side of the road. Flicking the torch on, she shone the light along the side of the old building. Sure enough, there was a small box at the side of the porch where she'd been told to find the key. Lifting the lid, she pulled out an envelope and flashed the torch on the spidery writing.

'*Henderson. Five nights.*' She shook the envelope and a large key slipped into her hand. Thank goodness, it was the right Beachside Vista, but it was *nothing* like she'd expected. It was definitely not the house in the ad.

143

No matter; it was close to the beach and that's where she'd be spending most of her time. Jilly shrugged and climbed the stairs. The door opened slowly with an ominous creak.

Talk about a cinematic setting. What was it going to be like inside?

Two minutes later—because that's all it took to investigate every nook and cranny of the *not-*spacious cottage—Jilly returned to the car for her backpack and food supplies. She quickly stowed her groceries in the ancient, rusted fridge on the back porch, along with the chocolate and the two bottles of wine she'd brought from her fridge at home. The plum pudding took pride of place in the centre of the old red laminated kitchen table and the red and green ribbon around it gave a small, festive air to the room.

The fridge was on the porch because there was no room in the tiny kitchen for much more than the table and two old mismatched chairs.

*Luxury?* Huh! She could cope with the décor but wasn't so sure about the outside shower and toilet located at the far end of the back porch. Jilly reached for the salad bag and closed the fridge. The bag crinkled in her hand as she looked down at the unappetizing green leaves. Changing her mind, she pulled open the door again, put the salad back, and pulled out a chocolate bar and a bottle of strawberry milk.

It was Christmas Eve, after all!

This would be her celebratory dinner, and then she'd brave a quick shower outside and have an early night. Look on the bright side; the cottage *was* cutesy in a retro kind of way, although she wondered how secure the back wall of the kitchen was. It was made entirely of latticework and wouldn't keep anything out.

Wind, bugs *or* intruders. And it was swaying in the wind with an ominous creak.

With a deep sigh and a swig of strawberry milk, Jilly searched out a clean towel from the mothball-smelling linen cupboard beside the back door and headed for the shower.

\*\*\*

Dominic pulled the cap off a bottle of beer and held the cool glass against his forehead. The air was muggy and by the look of the flashing sky and the rumbling to the west there was a decent night storm brewing. He took a swig of the beer, put it on the bench and picked up his keys. He'd clear out the carport and get the Audi under shelter as best he could. There was hail in that sky.

His eyes narrowed as he stepped outside. There was a light on in Derro's cottage down the road. There shouldn't be; no one had lived in their grandparents' place since Derro had died. Aunty Vi had talked about letting it as a holiday rental, but Dominic had convinced her not to. It hadn't taken much talking; as well as the physical problems with the place, the whole family knew the real reason it couldn't be let out.

*Not that we ever talk about it.*

With a sigh, he shoved his hands in his pockets and hurried down the steps. The last thing he wanted to do was go to the cottage, but he should make sure squatters hadn't moved in. All he wanted was peace and quiet for this break; he didn't want to have to deal with any problems.

Or any other person for that matter. He was here to surf and chill and forget about the cutthroat business world he'd left behind in Sydney.

##

Taking a shower in the tiny cubicle had been fraught with problems. Jilly had to manoeuvre an old surfboard out of the small shower recess and brush down the sticky cobwebs that hung from the showerhead to the taps on the wall. No sign of spiders but they could be lurking in the dark. At least the room looked clean, but the smell of mouldy concrete pervaded the dimly lit space. She reached up to open the small louvre window at the top of the shower and squealed as a Daddy Long

Legs spider scurried across her hand. She shook it off and opted to keep the window half-shut rather than brave the spider and any family he might have.

Slipping her shorts and T-shirt off, she looked around for somewhere to hang her clothes . . . and her towel. Not a hook or a bench to be seen. Opening the door a crack, she shoved them through the gap and placed them on the floor of the verandah, before turning on the taps and waiting. She jumped as another flash of lightning lit the night sky, and a far-off rumble of thunder reverberated along the verandah.

A clanking and groaning preceded the burst of steaming hot water that sprayed her from above. Jilly jumped back and it took a bit of fiddling to adjust the heat to a comfortable level, but finally she tipped her head back, and closed her eyes, letting the warm water ease her tension.

She was here; the inside of the cottage was clean; the bed was soft, and the beach was a stone's throw across the road. She had food and books to read and a couple of bikinis. What more could she need? This outside bathroom would add to the adventure. She opened her eyes and reached for the shampoo bottle on the floor and tipped it into her hand, lathering her long hair into sweet-smelling suds as a picture of sun-tipped curls came to mind.

What were the chances of running into her boss

in a small town so far from Sydney? He was the last person she would ever have expected to see in a pair of boardshorts. She narrowed her eyes as she remembered the sand on the back of his legs. Maybe he wasn't travelling; maybe he was staying in this beachside village although she doubted if there were any flash condos in this town.

Smooth golden skin filled her thoughts as she massaged her hair and imagined massaging those delectable muscles.

*Stop it.*

No matter how attracted she was to Mr. Dominic Smythe-Phillips, that attraction would be firmly put in its place when she went back to the office. Two work relationships had already gone pear-shaped and Jilly had sworn off them for life. Brad Wallace had used her to get a promotion at the Federal Bank and then suggested she move on when he'd been promoted above her. Luckily, the job at SAB had paid more and given her many more opportunities in the two years she'd been there.

Thanks for the opportunity, *Brad*.

Jilly closed her eyes as she rinsed the suds from her hair.

Phil Long had been worse; there was the wife he'd neglected to mention. Luckily Jilly had found out about her just in time.

So, the new policy she stuck to rigidly: work

and sex did not mix. Trouble was, working so hard, and looking after Dad left no time for meeting guys anywhere else.

Celibacy had been the order of her life for a long year.

*Creak.*

Jilly's eyes flew open as the sound of slow footsteps on the wooden verandah reached her. Quickly rinsing the last of the shampoo from her hair, she switched off the taps and listened. With her heart thudding madly, she opened the door a crack, bent down and reached for the towel. Her hand met smooth, worn floorboards and she stretched her arm out further and patted around the floor. There was no towel beneath her roving fingertips.

*Shit.* Or clothes. Pulling the door closed quietly, she listened as the front steps creaked.

*Great.* As she stood there wondering what the hell to do, someone pounded on the back door along the porch. She held her breath; if she was quiet maybe they'd go away. For goodness sake, she was bare-assed naked. When she slowly turned the lock on the inside of the shower door the resulting snick was like a gunshot going off.

*So much for trying to keep quiet.*

"Hello? Who's there? Where are you?"

"Oh, shit." She'd know that voice anywhere.

Jilly rolled her eyes as the deep and sexy voice of Mr. Iceberg drifted through the louvre window.

"Me."

"Who?" His voice was terse now, more like the impatient tones as he queried a report at the office.

"Er . . . I'm in here," she called out.

The footsteps came closer. Jilly leaned against the door and stifled a groan.

*Of all the rotten luck.*

"Where's here and who's me?" His voice was louder, and she leaned back against the wall and rubbed her arms. The wind was swirling through the gap above the door now and goose bumps rose on her bare, wet skin.

"In the shower." She realised he would have no idea where the shower was. "At the end of the verandah. And it's me, Jilly Henderson."

Silence.

*What the hell is he doing here anyway?* She stood there shivering as cold rivulets of water ran down from her wet hair to her neck and body. Taking a deep breath, she tried to compose herself. Her nipples gave a little tug before flaring to high beam, ready to say hello to anyone who looked.

*Blasted cold.*

Jilly had no intention of stepping out of this shower until she had a towel around her and her clothes back from wherever they were.

"Jilly?"

"Yes, it's me."

"What the hell are you doing in there?" The sexy voice had taken on a dangerous edge now. It appeared he was just as unimpressed to find her here, as she was to hear him outside the shower. "I'm taking a shower.

"Why are you here? Did you follow me?"

"Why the hell would I do that?"

If he wanted to play nasty, she could be cranky too. She wasn't at work and she didn't have to put up with his stiff manner like she did most days at work. A tight smile with a muttered good morning was as social and pleasant as he got in the office. Even if he looked sexy when he smiled, he never made friendly overtures to anyone. Hence the Mr. Iceberg tag.

But she was at a disadvantage here.

At least he had clothes on. Well, some clothes anyway. Her nipples tightened as the memory of that golden sun-kissed skin flashed through her mind again.

"Well, what *are* you doing here?'

"I t*old* you. I was taking a shower." Her voice was as cold as her skin which was now completely covered with goose bumps. Strange, because the evening was hot and muggy. A cool breeze rushed through the shower and the back of Jilly's neck

151

prickled. A chuckle sounded from the other side of the shower door.

"What's so funny?" Indignation filled her at the thought of Dominic Smythe-Phillips standing outside laughing at her predicament.

*Wait a minute.* Her eyes narrowed. The only way he would know of her predicament would be if *he'd* moved her clothes and towel.

Another voice came from the other end of the verandah and Jilly strained to hear. There was someone with him. A shiver of fear snaked up her spine.

Don't be stupid, it's only Dominic—the storm was making her skittish.

"Dominic? Look I need some help here." But all she heard was that same quiet chuckle a little closer this time.

"Dominic!" Her voice was shrill as she pushed away the fear that was settling in her chest. There was nothing to be afraid of. This was Dominic Smythe-Phillips, second-in-charge of the largest trading bank in Sydney and a well-respected businessman . . . and her boss. She sat outside his office and spoke to him every day.

Okay, so she didn't know much about him— never a personal conversation—but his quietly spoken demeanour and his rare, albeit sexy, smile told her he was a decent guy. Although he was distant, he was always polite, never lost his temper and had never seemed the sort to play a practical joke.

*Like taking my clothes.* Another shiver ran down her back and she leaned against the shower wall.

"If you're here, go away. Okay?" Dominic's whisper was quiet and the floorboards on the verandah creaked again.

*If* you're here? Who else was there?

Jilly looked around the small shower cubicle for something to cover up with but there was nothing there apart from the soap and shampoo bottle.

That would be a great look, she thought. Charge out with a cake of soap over one boob and a bottle of shampoo over the other.

*Ta da! Hello Dominic!*

A door slammed somewhere outside.

"Just stop it!" His voice was angry now.

"Stop what?" Jilly called out. "Look, I . . . I need a hand in here." *Oh, damn it.* "I . . . I don't mean a hand, I mean I need some help."

"I didn't say that." By the close sound of his voice Dominic was outside the shower now.

"Say what?" It was like some sort of bizarre movie, nothing was making sense, least of all this conversation. "Look, Dominic . . . I mean, Mr.

Smythe-Phillips"—keep it formal or as formal as she could, naked and no clothes within reach— "I don't know what you're playing at, but I would be very grateful if you would pass my clothes in."

*And then go away.*

"What clothes?"

Jilly gritted her teeth. "The clothes and towel you took from outside the shower."

This time she could hear the amusement in his voice. "So, you're in there in your er . . . shall I say . . . in your natural glory?"

So he *could* crack a joke but she was decidedly unimpressed.

"I am in here, waiting for you to return my towel and clothes." Jilly folded her arms across her chest. Her skin was drying rapidly in the cool breeze blowing through the half-open slats of the louvre window. She was not finding this situation the slightest bit amusing, like her boss seemed to be.

"I'm sorry. I don't have them."

Jilly couldn't figure out the tone of his voice.

There was another hurried whisper. "I didn't take them.'

"Who else is out there?" She folded her arms.

"No one."

*Bullshit.*

Another nervous skitter ran up her back. "Well,

if you didn't take them can you please find them? A pair of shorts and a T-shirt, and a pink towel." The thought of him finding her undies blowing about the lawn brought heat to her cheeks.

"They must have blown away. There's a nasty storm brewing. I'll go and look down in the yard."

Receding footsteps, soft whispers and then silence. There *was* someone else there with him.

When she'd looked at the Audi at the gas station, Jilly hadn't noticed anyone else with him. But then, she admitted to herself, she'd been too busy perving on his butt to take much notice of anything else. She bit back a groan and reached up to squeeze some of the water from her hair while she waited.

# Chapter Four

There was no sign of clothes or a towel on the verandah, or in the long grass at the back of the house. Not that Dominic expected to find them there. He'd felt like an idiot trying to talk to someone who he really didn't believe was there, but Aunty Vi always said—

*Shit.* Forget about that. He had thought he'd heard a laugh . . . and seen . . . something. Maybe it was just the wind and the moonlight.

His suspicions as to where the clothes had gone were crazy so he wouldn't be sharing them with Jilly Henderson. She'd think he was a total fruit cake if he shared that thought with her. He also wanted to know why the hell she was in Derro's cottage and how long she thought she was staying there. But the way things were shaping up, he suspected she'd be out of there at daylight. Or at least Dominic hoped she would but that created another problem. The town was always booked out from Christmas to mid-January so there'd be no accommodation left.

*How the hell had she ended up at the cottage?* At the gas station, he'd assumed Jilly would be heading to Byron Bay, or even the Gold Coast. This town was for retirees and surfers; there was nothing sophisticated to do here. And that was how he'd always found her.

*Sophisticated and distant.* The casually dressed Miss Henderson in the gas station had rocked him.

Dominic came back up the steps and looked around. The breeze had dropped, and the air was still. The chill that had pervaded the verandah a moment ago had gone.

*Good.*

"Look," he said. "I'm sorry, but I can't find them. The wind must have carried them further than I can see. I can get a torch and go looking further."

"No, thank you. Just go."

"Do you want me to go inside and get you another towel?" He stood outside the door.

"No." The retort was immediate and definite.

"So . . . a nudie run?" The image that flashed though his mind made him want to hang around for the show.

"No!"

Dominic bit back a grin; he wondered what

157

she intended doing. A nudie run would be worth seeing. Her staid black corporate suit had well disguised the lush curves the brief shorts and clinging T-shirt had accentuated. The tightly pulled-back chignon had given no hint to the gorgeous red curls that cascaded down Miss Henderson's back to that delicious rounded butt.

He folded his arms and leaned back on the rail. "So how can I help?"

"Go away and I'll go inside after you've gone."

"No, I want to talk to you."

"Well, talk away."

His lips tilted. This little spitfire was very different to his quiet executive assistant from the office. A southward rush of blood had one part of him very interested.

"How about I go around to the other end of the verandah, and when you're dressed you can come out and we can talk?"

"How will I know you've gone?" Her voice was wary.

"Because I'm a gentleman and I'm going now. I'll keep my back turned." He pushed away from the railing regretfully. "Promise."

"All right then. No peeking."

"No peeking." Sometimes being a man of his word had its disadvantages, but he wasn't a voyeur. Dominic walked to the end of the verandah and looked across the road to the beach, keeping his back to the small outside bathroom.

The north-easterly wind had picked up and, as dark as it was, he could still see the white caps whipped up out to sea when the lightning flashed. The wind whistled through the trees lining the edge of the road and the first spits of rain landed at the edge of the verandah. He looked up; the clouds were low and scudding fast. If he stayed here much longer, he was in for a soaking on the way home.

A door banged behind him and he turned around slowly.

He couldn't help the grin as he met the wide-eyed gaze of one very naked woman. One very *beautiful* naked woman. Jilly was tugging on the handle of the back door at the other end of the verandah.

Her eye met his as she dropped her hands to cover herself.

"Turn around," she squealed. "Now!"

Being the gentleman he was—*damn it*—Dominic let the appreciative smile slide as he swung his gaze away.

"The door slammed shut in front of me just as I was about to go in." Indignation seemed to have overcome her embarrassment. Her tone made it sound as though she was holding him responsible.

From the brief glimpse of long, slender limbs

and the verification that she was indeed a natural redhead, Dominic wanted to reassure Jilly she certainly had nothing to be embarrassed about. But embarrassment didn't seem to be on the top of her list. Without looking, he could feel the glare she was directing to him. He bit back a smile. His Miss Henderson was becoming more interesting by the minute.

"Who's here with you?" Her voice was cross now. "Are they inside the cottage?"

"Nobody. I'm here by myself."

"Bullshit." The prim and proper executive assistant *had* long gone. "I heard you talking to someone."

"Uh uh, must have been the wind. There's a fair storm brewing. Look"— Dominic went to turn around and remembered just in time— "you scurry back into the shower, I'll unlock the door, cover my eyes and then you can go inside."

"All right," she said slowly.

"And then we'll talk about *why* you're here."

Five minutes later, things had gone according to his plan. Dominic had managed to get the door open; it hadn't been locked, just jammed shut. He'd dutifully turned his back again while Jilly scurried past. Now she stood at the door dressed in a pair of shorts and a singlet top, her wet curls plastered to the sides of her face. Dominic's fingers itched to reach out and lift the wet strands from her skin, but he didn't think she would appreciate it. Ushering him inside, she pointed to one of the chairs at the old kitchen table—Dominic grinned, the same wooden ones that had been there since he was a kid.

"Now explain." Her voice was short, and her cheeks were flushed. "Did you follow me here?"

He ignored the chair and shook his head. "Where from? Sydney?"

She let out an exasperated sigh. "No, the gas station."

"Why would I do that?" Leaning instead against the old bench top, he folded his arms, watching with fascination as a single droplet of water landed on her shoulder and slowly ran down towards the neckline of her tight T-shirt. "You're the one with the explaining to do, not me. What are *you* doing here? Did you follow me from the gas station?"

"What am I doing here?" Her voice rose with each word. "I'm staying here for my Christmas break."

"No, you're not."

"And why would that be, Mr. Smythe-Phillips?" Her voice was laced with saccharine-sweetness and Dominic bit back a smile. If it hadn't been for the fact that she couldn't stay here, he would have quite enjoyed spending a few days getting to know this very different Miss Henderson. This little red-headed kitten was showing her sharp claws and he waited for the reaction which was sure to come when he told her she definitely *wasn't* staying here. He shrugged, putting on a casual air.

"It's my family's cottage and we don't rent it out. You're squatting."

"Squatting!"

"Yep, squatting. How did you get in?"

"With the key!"

"You're still squatting. You'll have to go."

"Be that as it may"—she turned around and picked up a scrunched piece of paper from the table— "this says that I can rent it . . . and I am. I'm not going anywhere. I don't care who owns it. I have a *receipt*."

Dominic folded his arms and leaned against the wall ignoring the piece of paper she held out to him.

"No," he said.

Jilly took a step closer to Dominic and eyeballed him. "Yes," she said.

Their eyes met and held; he ignored the little jolt that raced through him as he stared at the golden flecks in her green eyes. They tipped at the corners and were beautiful; he'd never noticed them behind the square, dark spectacles she wore in the office.

"You can't."

"I can."

Mexican standoff. Okay, how could he handle this without looking like a complete fool? Dominic lifted his head as a fleeting shimmer of light flickered briefly. He stared at the wall with a frown and waited for a noise or . . . or something. *He* wasn't used to this yet, so how the hell could he explain it to a stranger?

He shook his head with a frown. It must have been the lightning. If he wasn't careful, he'd end up as crazy as Derro's sister. Thinking quickly, he gathered together the most persuasive argument he could come up with.

"Look, Jilly. Is it okay if I call you that?" He pulled out the best grin he could. "I'm more used to calling you Miss Henderson, but it is the holiday season."

She nodded, hands on hips, chin thrust forward. "You may, Mr. Smythe-Phillips." Despite her belligerent stance, the nod was cool and regal.

So, it was like that was it? She was a tough player in the bank, and it looked like she was going to be as tough to deal with personally.

"I'm really sorry, but you can't stay here. There's been a mistake. This place has been in my family for years and it's in no fit state to be let out. Just take a look around." Dominic ran his hand through his salt-encrusted hair. He'd slipped into town for beer and petrol after he'd been surfing and probably wasn't dressed in a way that would assist his position here as a sort of landlord. "You could get hurt and you could sue us. I don't know how you were able to rent it."

"It was in my staff email. 'Retro holiday cottage on north coast, available to SBA staff only.' I checked it out online, talked to the guy at the phone number given, paid in full by cheque and here I am." She narrowed her eyes as she held the receipt out to him. "To stay."

"What guy? What was his name?" Dominic stared back at her. Her cheeks were flushed.

"Derek somebody."

*Bloody hell.*

Dominic shook his head slowly. "Look, I don't know how it's happened but there's been a mistake. There is no Derek. You can't stay here. The place is falling down. Look around you. It's in no fit state for guests."

God knew what could happen here during the night. All he knew was, he wouldn't sleep here, and he wasn't about to let a woman—albeit a very attractive woman—sleep here alone. "I'll find you a motel room somewhere."

"No."

"I'll pay for it."

"No."

Dominic should have known the tenacity that

had got Jilly Henderson to the position of executive assistant before she was thirty would make her dig her heels in. Yes, he knew how old she was; despite the staff thinking he sat up in some ivory tower, he knew everything there was to know about his executive team. She'd graduated with her MBA a couple of years ago, had recently celebrated her twenty-eighth birthday and lived alone on the lower north shore, not too far from his apartment. As far as he knew she was single; her personal life never intruded on her work at the office and she rarely attended office social functions. His mind ticked over as she stared back at him.

Jilly's shoulders straightened. She walked across to the door and held it open. "Look, Dominic. Is it okay if I call you that?" She parroted his words as she pulled the door open. This time it opened smoothly beneath her hands without the sign of a creak. He stepped through as she ushered him outside with a flick of her hand.

"I'm not a guest, I'm a paying tenant. I don't care about the state of the cottage and don't worry, I won't sue you. I've had a long drive, I'm tired and I want to go to bed." She stepped back and stared at him, obviously waiting for him to leave. "I have no idea why you are here too. However, I do appreciate your concern. Thank you and good night."

Dominic stood on the dark verandah and

opened his mouth to speak.

"I'll see you in January," Jilly said.

The door closed in his face.

# Chapter Five

*Christmas Day*

Despite the booming thunder when Jilly finally climbed into bed, she slept soundly and dreamlessly. Mr. Persistent Smythe-Phillips had finally given up trying to persuade her to leave through the closed door.

"If you have any problems through the night—*any*—I'm in the cottage up the road," he said, finally accepting that she was here to stay. "Don't hesitate to call me."

"Don't worry, I'm not the litigious type," she'd called through the door. What a bizarre conversation to be having on Christmas Eve with her boss. She still couldn't believe he was here at this isolated beach.

She had seen a completely different side to him as he had done his best to move her out of the cottage, but she'd stood firm. This was *her* holiday and she wasn't going anywhere unless he could come up with a better reason than the cottage wasn't suitable, according to him.

*Dangerous! Pfft.* The only dangerous things she'd come across so far were one Daddy Long Legs spider . . . and an altogether too sexy boss.

She shook her head at Dominic being here in this small town. Was it a coincidence? He would have been the last person she'd ever expect to run into in a small beachside village like this. If she'd known the cottage belonged to his family, she would never have rented it. But she had and she was here to stay. Sitting up, Jilly stretched her arms high and looked around. Sunlight was pouring in through the lacy, white nylon curtains at the bedroom window. The storm had died out as she'd drifted off to sleep, snug in the soft bed. The timber walls were painted a soft yellow and the brightness of the room buoyed her mood.

She slid her legs over the side of the bed onto the timber floor. The worn boards were smooth beneath her bare feet as she headed outside to have a wash. A light breakfast, slip into her bikini and sarong, and then hit the beach. A relaxing day of reading and chilling out beckoned.

Time to face her grief and move on. That's what Dad would have wanted her to do. He would have been pleased to know that she'd chosen to spend Christmas here; he could never understand her trips to Bali, Vanuatu and other overseas tropical destinations.

'Look in your own backyard, sweetheart. Our beaches on the north coast are the best in the world.'

Doing what she knew Dad would have approved of, had eased her grief a little. She focused on the happy memories of him teaching her to surf at Narrabeen in the days before life got too hectic to enjoy. When Mum had been alive, and they had been a family.

Tears threatened as she headed for the outside loo. She'd let herself have a good cry one night, and then move on. It was extra tough this year because it was Christmas and she had no family left.

After she'd washed, Jilly stood at the lounge window and had a quick snack of fruit and another full-cream strawberry milk—*sorry hips*—she'd go for a long walk later. The sea air had kicked in and she was hungrier than usual. If she stood on her tiptoes, she could just catch a glimpse of the deep blue water through the she-oaks fringing the sand across the road. Last night's storm had washed everything clean; she pushed the window up and drew in a deep breath of salt-laden air. Peace stole over her and Jilly couldn't help the big grin that crossed her face.

Eight whole days of solitude and bliss ahead— no frantic trading and no emails that must be acted upon immediately.

She put her dishes in the pink porcelain kitchen sink. But although tired and dated, everything in the place was in good condition and clean. She shook her head remembering Dominic's agitation last night. He was worrying about nothing; the cottage was old, but fine. She smiled; it *was* retro in an original sort of way. He could sort out the rental issue with his family; it wasn't her problem.

As she pulled up the bedcovers, something slid from the end of the bed and Jilly bent to pick it up. She held the unfamiliar plastic bag in her hand and frowned as she turned it over in her hands. She was sure it hadn't been on the bed last night. She opened the bag and peered into it and her frown deepened. The shorts, T-shirt and towel, and undies which she'd assumed had blown off the verandah last night were folded neatly inside.

*What the* . . .

After Dominic had left, she had gone outside with her torch and searched around the long grass and beneath the low verandah but there'd been no sign of her clothes. How the hell did they get into a bag *and* onto her bed through the night? She put the bag aside and folded her arms, her temper building.

What the hell was he playing at? How *dare* he come into the cottage while she was sleeping? The cottage belonged to his family; he must have

170

another key.

Well, she'd be paying Mr. Smythe-Phillips a visit and telling him to stay away from her. While she was on vacation she didn't have to kowtow to his imperious demands.

##

Jilly detoured via the cottage up the road on her way to the beach. Slipping her beach bag over her shoulder, she passed Dominic's silver Audi. It was parked in a small lean-to on the side of the other cottage. She climbed the stairs identical to the ones at her cottage, took a deep breath and pounded on the front door. This cottage was the same design as the one she was staying in. The same coloured paint peeling from the exterior weatherboards and a small bathroom on the far end of the verandah. Her legs were trembling as she practiced her prepared speech. She cleared her throat.

*Stay right away from the cottage and from me.* The shakiness in her legs, and the funny curling feeling in the pit of her stomach had nothing to do with the anticipation of seeing him again.

*No way.*

Jilly dug deep to bring back the anger that had coursed through her when she had realised that he had been in her bedroom while she was sleeping.

*Ergh.* Forget the anticipation that was skittering

171

through her. It was almost creepy; Dominic had certainly conned them at the bank with his gentle and polite manner.

All was silent inside the house, and she pounded on the door again. Perversely, she hoped he was sleeping, and she pounded harder, hoping she'd wake him up. But after a third go of trying to raise the dead with her curled fist on the timber door, all remained silent. Jilly stood there for a moment, biting her lip, before she shrugged and turned away to walk to the beach.

He'd keep till later.

She drew in a gasp of delight as she stepped through the row of she-oaks fringing the sand. Sapphire blue water filled her vision for as far as she could see, and the morning sun sparkled on the water. Snowy-white cumulo-nimbus clouds sat low above the far horizon in the distance, the same color as the foam on the breaking waves that rolled into the beach. The long, lazy swells rolling in across the Pacific steepened and broke into gentle waves as the ocean floor bottomed out, before they pushed up the white sandy shore.

Dad was right. This was one of the most beautiful beaches she'd ever seen. And it was almost deserted.

Far away in the distance, a couple walked ahead of a dog frolicking in the shallows. The rest of the beach was clear, with not another soul in sight. Jilly scanned the sand looking for a spot to settle in for the morning. She'd lathered herself in sunscreen after she'd slipped into her white bikini and had a wide-brimmed hat to protect her face. Her Kindle was charged, and she'd packed two bottles of cold water in her beach bag. She spread her towel on the sand and glanced up as a movement in the water caught her eye. A lone surfer was surfing the point a little to the north. Jilly straightened and put her hand to her eyes with an envious sigh.

Rising gracefully to his feet he turned when his board picked up the front of the wave. He glided effortlessly through the translucent water, so clear she could see the back of the board as he gained speed down the face of the wave. She held her breath as the wave curled over him and he disappeared into the tube for a few seconds before shooting out triumphantly from the right-hand break.

Clapping her hands, Jilly smiled as he turned and paddled back to catch the next wave. It had been a long time since Dad had taught her to surf; she'd spent a lot of time on a board at Narrabeen when she was in her teens. She had never forgotten the power of pushing her board across and down the face of the wave at the same time; the adrenaline rush of the speed combined with the thrill of the movement. Being at one with nature—feeling the air, hearing the whoosh and suck of the wave as water sprayed around you, there was nothing like it.

Lately life had passed her by, and she'd been focused on work and Dad's health, and she'd taken little time for herself.

A good New Year's resolution.
*Jilly time 2020!*

By the time the surfer caught the next wave she'd settled on her towel and pushed the sand into a mound behind her back to lean on as she read. She narrowed her eyes as the wave pushed him closer to the section of the beach where she was sitting. With a groan, she looked away and picked up her Kindle; she should have known it was Dominic.

But as much as she tried to focus on her book, she couldn't stop looking up and watching as he caught wave after wave in a show of effortless manoeuvres. Finally, she gave up and laced her fingers behind the back of her head and gave in to sheer admiration. Who would ever have known that the staid boss of the SAB could carve up a wave like that? He was an absolute pro, as good as any she'd ever watched. A couple of times, Jilly caught her breath as his board teetered on the edge of the wave before he turned and sliced across the face of it. Finally, he caught a wave and paddled to the shore.

She pulled her hat low over her face, quickly picked up her Kindle and rolled over onto her stomach as he walked up the beach. Hopefully he wouldn't notice her on the way back.

Five minutes later, cold water splashed onto the backs of her legs; her hope had been futile. She rolled over and leaned back on her elbows, squinting up into the bright sunshine.

"Morning, Jilly." Dominic rested his board on the sand and Jilly looked away as he squatted beside her, that golden-tanned chest way too close for her comfort.

"Good morning." She looked away from that magnificent expanse of bare skin, pleased that her sunglasses hid her expression. She pointed to the surf as the next wave crashed onto the beach.

"Pretty impressive surfing."

"You sound surprised." Dominic tipped his head to the side, obviously to clear the water from his ears. Jilly looked up at him as water droplets flew from his wet curls. His eyelashes were salt-encrusted, and his blue eyes were alight with the smile that crossed his face as he stared back at her. His face was tanned, contrasting with the white zinc cream smeared on his nose. He could have passed for an eighteen-year-old; his grin was cheeky, and he looked relaxed and happy.

"I am. It's the last thing I expected to see you doing," she said honestly trying to keep her eyes from his muscled chest. "I'm used to you sitting at a desk in a suit firing orders at me." She flicked a hand towards his board. "Doesn't suit the corporate image I had." Although that image *had* shimmied away last night when she'd seen him in his boardshorts at the gas station.

"You should try it sometime. Nothing like it." He stared out at the sea. "I grew up here and the surf was my life before I left for uni."

Surprise ran through Jilly. She'd always thought he's come from the north shore of Sydney. Silver spoon and all that.

"I know. I love it too." Jilly couldn't help smiling back. "I surfed at Narrabeen when I was at high school."

Dominic grinned at her and her heart did a little flip flop in her chest. She put her hand to her mouth pretending to yawn, forgetting all her previous thoughts of his strange behaviour. The top of his wetsuit had been pulled down and she stared at the glistening water drops on his chest. Despite the bright sun, she could see the frown that suddenly wrinkled his high forehead.

"Did you sleep well?" His tone was probing, and his words jerked her out of that silly adolescent mooning.

"I did. *Unfortunately*." She killed the smile as it all came flooding back and stared. "And apparently I slept a little too deeply."

"Why?" His voice was cautious. "What do you mean by that?"

"Look, I've calmed down a bit now."

*How to put this politely but make her point very clear?*

"I went to your cottage to see you on the way here and I was pretty angry."

"Because?"

"Because I don't appreciate you just letting yourself into my cottage whenever you feel like it. I don't care if the place belongs to your family. If it happens again, I'll—"

"Whoa. Just wait one minute. You think I was there while you were asleep? That's sick. No way did I—or would I ever do that."

His expression and the horrified indignation in his tone convinced her immediately he was telling the truth.

"Well, who else would put my clothes into a plastic bag and leave them on the end of my bed? Do you provide a maid service in your holiday rentals?" Her tone was sarcastic, but she wanted an answer. If he hadn't put them there, who had?

"Trust me." Dominic stared at her and his voice

was soft. He balanced on the balls of his feet and looked away from her out to the sea as he ran his hand through his hair. "I believe you, but I just want you to know that I did not—and would not—come into your cottage uninvited. It wasn't me. My cousin, Margaret, has a key. Maybe she found them?"

Jilly pushed herself to her feet and brushed the loose sand from her legs. He'd been too close for her comfort in the sand beside her. "Okay, if you say so, I guess I'll take your word for it."

He stood and she tipped her head to the side and looked at him curiously. Even though he had denied it and she had no reason not to believe him, he still looked ill at ease.

"Okay, if it wasn't your cousin, maybe I just had a memory lapse or something." She reached out to touch his arm in an attempt to lighten the tension. "I've had a tough few days and I'm pretty tired. I really needed this break. My boss works me very hard, you know." She let a tentative smile cross her face. He looked so concerned she felt bad.

"Thank you." Dominic straightened his shoulders and Jilly had to tip her head back to keep eye contact. "Have you given any more thought about moving to a motel?"

Jilly put her hands on her hips and jutted her chin out as any sympathy fled.

# Chapter Six

Dominic looked down at the woman staring at him. He knew very well how hard Jilly Henderson worked, and he was just sorry that the chances of her having a restful Christmas in that cottage were slim. He stared down at her beautiful green eyes as they locked with his. A man could drown in them. He'd not been immune to her at the office, but he had tried to ignore it. Even though she was quiet and professional in her dealings with him, he'd often heard her laughter coming from the morning tea room as she'd chatted to the other staff. But she'd always kept a barrier up between them and it had rankled, even though avoiding office romances was a policy he'd stuck to religiously as he'd climbed the corporate pole. Too many issues in the business world were generated by office relationships after a fling. Friday night staff drinks were notorious for beginning relationships between staff that were committed elsewhere.

And it always happened at this time of the year;

another reason to avoid the Christmas drinks that seemed to be on every night from the first of December until the big office party when there was inevitably a tale of woe. Staff turnover from the Christmas party fallout was a given every year.

*But not for him.*

"Earth to Dominic." Jilly's familiar voice washed over him. He ignored the little jolt that headed for his groin but was thankful that he was wearing boardshorts over his budgie smugglers. The budgie had already given a little chirp when Jilly's hand had touched his arm a moment ago.

"Sorry. You had me back in the office for a while there. And yes, I do know how hard you work." He wasn't going to mention someone being in in her cottage—if she was prepared to put it down to a memory lapse, he wasn't going to discourage it. But he was going to do his damnedest to make sure it didn't happen again.

*If I had a bloody clue how to, that is.*

"So, seeing your boss is such a hard taskmaster, he needs to make sure you have a great holiday. How would you like to come for a surf with me in the morning?" Dominic couldn't take his eyes off Jilly when her face broke into a wide smile. She was drop dead *gorgeous*. And if he kept his eyes on her face, his gaze wasn't tempted to stray to the luscious curves packaged in that white bikini.

"Oh, yes please! That'd be awesome. Do you have a spare board?"

"I do, but I'm pretty sure we'll find a smaller one to suit you in the shed at the back of your cottage. It shouldn't be locked. I'll come down and have a look this afternoon if that's okay?" He waited for her nod. After last night's antics, he wasn't going to go near the place and give her any reason to doubt him. As far as he knew all his and Derro's boards had been there for years. He was the only one of all the cousins who ever came back to the coast. Except for Margaret; she'd never moved away. The rest of them were scattered far and wide over the world in a variety of careers. One thing he could say about the Smythe-Phillips; they were all high achievers.

Except for Derro, but maybe he'd known what life was going to hold for him.

Dominic gazed out over the ocean; Derro had never had a career goal. Surfing had been his life and it had caused his death before he was twenty. His ashes had been scattered to the wind on this very beach ten years ago. Guilt ran through him; he hadn't caught up with Margaret for years. She'd been the older, crazy cousin as they'd grown up and run wild at their grandparents' beach cottages and Derro's death had tipped her into eccentricity. When he'd last seen her, he'd been shocked at how much she'd aged.

Despite the sadness that came with being here, Dominic had looked forward to coming home. This was the place he could be himself and not the corporate suit that he'd turned into. He had planned to use this week as a time to reconsider his future. His current life was not what he wanted for himself, even if he was making a success of it. Maybe it was time for a change; a sea change. Even after only two nights away from Sydney, peace was stealing through his bones. But he certainly didn't need the complication of anyone in that cottage and the problems it could bring.

That person was now staring up at him with a strange expression on her face.

Jilly reached out again and touched his arm gently. "Dominic?"

"Yes?" He gave his head a gentle shake. She had a terrible effect on him; his thoughts were all over the place.

"Merry Christmas."

"Oh. I forgot. And to you too." A chuckle accompanied his words. "How about when I come over, I bring a couple of beers and we can sit on your porch and watch the storm after we dig out a board for you?" He'd had no intention of saying that and his words surprised him. At least if he was there, he could keep her safe. Not that he thought she could really come to any harm. After all what could—

"Storm?" Jilly frowned at him and lifted her eyes to the clear blue sky.

"Guaranteed to be a storm later." Dominic lifted his head and sniffed the pure air. "Can't you smell it?"

Jilly's pretty laugh trilled around him. "No, I can't, but I'll take your word for it. And yes, it would be nice to have some company."

Despite her laugh, he was surprised to see a tear drop from the tip of her long eyelashes. He reached out and used the pad of his thumb to wipe it from her cheek.

"You okay?"

She let out an unladylike sniff and wiped her hand over her eyes. "Sorry. First Christmas without my dad. I thought I'd be okay, but I guess I'm not."

"Nothing to be sorry about. It's tough, isn't it? What about your mum?"

Jilly shook her head mutely.

He stared over her head to the ocean and let her gather herself together.

"I lost both my parents in the same year. It's hard. Times like Christmas and birthdays really bring it home," he said.

"Come on over later. When you're ready." A

small smile tilted her lips. "I'll try not to be rude to you this afternoon.'

Dominic picked up his board and hitched it beneath his arm. He was reluctant to go back to the cottage; he was enjoying her company. "Okay, sounds like a plan; I'll see you later." As he turned away, Dominic allowed himself one lingering glance at the lush curves in the white bikini.

*Yep, she's drop-dead gorgeous.*

Maybe his office rule could take a break too.

# Chapter Seven

Jilly didn't spend much longer on the beach; the summer sunshine was burning hot. With her fair skin, she'd end up looking like a lobster. It took her a while to get immersed in her book; the sight of Dominic walking away from her with the board beneath his arm, his strong muscles flexing, had set her heart in a little pitter patter, and it was hard to concentrate. Then she opened her Kindle and tried to focus on one of the romances she had downloaded. For a couple of hours, she buried herself in an imaginary world, not giving any thought to Dominic or the sorting out of Dad's stuff that waited for her back in Sydney.

Eventually, the hot sun—not to mention the steamy scenes in the romance—got too much and she packed up her bag and towel. The sexy romance about a holiday fling had her thoughts heading in an inappropriate direction.

A holiday fling? *Maybe that's what I need?*

*Uh, uh.* She shook her head. Not with her boss.

Although it *was* becoming harder to reconcile the Dominic of the surf with Mr. Smythe-Phillips of the office. Maybe it would help if he put a shirt on. Too much naked chest for her comfort.

*But what a gorgeous naked chest.*

Jilly grinned as she headed back to the beach house. She paused as she opened the gate to the path that led to the front door. Someone had mowed the grass and cleaned up the garden while she'd been at the beach. The cottage looked prettier with smooth, green lawn surrounding it; more like the photo in the email. The edges had been trimmed and the long grass outside the fence was neatly clipped too. She closed the gate behind her and took two steps before she stopped dead and looked around slowly, her mouth dropping open.

Her car was gone. Jilly spun on her heel and looked back to the road; no sign of it. She climbed the steps slowly and walked along the verandah to the door and her heart lodged in her throat. The door was wide open and the key she had locked it with was in her beach bag. She put her bag on the table outside the door and poked her head inside cautiously.

"Hello?" Her voice was husky, and she cleared her throat. "Dominic? Are you in there?" Her eyes settled on the small dining table. Her car keys were sitting exactly where she had left them last night.

But a small vase filled with pretty summer flowers was in the middle of the table.

Jilly frowned and backed out through the doorway before walking to the far end of the verandah and peering around the back of the house. She let out the breath she had been holding. Her little red sedan was parked behind the shed in the longer grass. Whoever had mowed had moved her car to the back. Folding her arms, she marched along the verandah and stepped back inside.

Thoughtful, but presumptuous.

"Is there anybody here?" Her temper was growing by the minute. If Dominic had wanted her to move her car so he could mow, all he'd had to do was ask. God, he knew she was on the beach; he could have waited till she came back.

How dare he just walk in, pick up her keys and move her car as though he owned the place? Well, in a way, he did. The place belonged to his family, but she was a tenant and she didn't feel at all comfortable with him having free access to where she was staying. She was tempted to march up and front him straight away, but she'd wait until he came down later.

Jilly picked up her Kindle, raided the fridge for a healthy snack and wandered back outside. She narrowed her eyes. In between the door and the shower halfway along the verandah, a small hammock chair hung from a hook. She walked up to it and gave it a gentle push as she looked around. She was sure that chair hadn't been there last night when she'd had her shower. She shrugged; it looked inviting, calico macramé knots held it together and colourful cushions invited her to sink in and curl her legs up.

Jilly backed into the hammock and sat cross-legged, testing the weight, before she leaned back against the soft cushions.

Okay, putting up a chair like this for her to chill in, maybe she could forgive him for coming by while she was at the beach. It *was* thoughtful to mow the lawn and move her car, so it didn't get chipped. Maybe he was just trying to make amends for being so insistent that she move to a motel.

Not a chance. She could see herself spending the rest of the week rocking in this chair reading. Putting one foot against the wooden rail at the edge of the verandah, she pushed hard, and the hammock rocked gently from side to side.

*Bliss.* Just what she needed.

Jilly flipped open the Kindle and began to read. She took a deep breath as the sexy scenes got hotter and hotter.

*Oh, my.*

She read until her eyelids began to droop, keen to keep reading as the story came to a searing climax. Finally, she put her Kindle aside and snuggled into the cushions for an afternoon nap. The only problem with the hammock was it wouldn't swing unless you pushed it, but Jilly was too comfy and she closed her eyes and let sleep overtake her.

## ##

*Creak, creak, creak.* The gentle swinging of the hammock chair soothed Jilly as she surfaced from the delicious realms of sleep a while later. She stretched and rubbed her eyes as the chair rocked from side to side; she'd had the most explicit dream about Dominic. A smile crossed her face; that's what she got for reading steamy romance novels. As she came fully awake, she stiffened. The chair was swinging from side to side as someone pushed it from behind.

*God, I dream about him and he turns up.*

"Dominic?"

No reply. The hammock swung away, and she had to hang onto the side to avoid falling out.

"That's so not funny." Jilly waited until the swinging slowed and putting her feet to the ground, she slid out of the chair. She really wasn't appreciating her boss's sense of humour. Putting her hands on her hips, she opened her mouth and stepped to the back of the chair. Goose bumps pricked her arms and the hair on the back of her neck rose as a coldness swept along the verandah.

*There was nobody there.* The chair was rocking by itself. Jilly closed her mouth and put her hand on the chair to stop it swinging. Deep in thought, she walked to the end of the small porch and looked up the road. There was no sign of anyone. The sky was clouding over but the air outside was still with the expectant hush before a storm. There was no birdsong and only the sound of the gentle whoosh of the waves breaking on the sand reached her.

It must have been the wind.

*But there is none.*

Maybe she'd done it herself as she'd been waking up?

Jilly turned as the silence was broken by the purr of a motor and Dominic's silver Audi cruised past. He lifted his arm in a wave but kept driving to his house further up the road.

*** 

Dominic narrowed his eyes as he waved to Jilly. The garden around the cottage had been cleaned up and the lawn mown.

*Nice of her to do that.* He'd intended offering to do it tomorrow, but she'd obviously found the old push mower in the shed while he'd been in town getting some snacks; he had a few beers in the fridge. Luckily the gas station where he'd run into her last night had opened for a few hours on the public holiday, and it had been deserted today. He drove into the small covered lean-to shed. The sky to the southwest was black with tinges of green with the promise of hail. They were in for a pearler of a storm this afternoon.

After taking a quick shower, he grabbed the six-pack of beer from the fridge and sauntered down the road. Anticipation filled him at the prospect of spending some time with Jilly.

Maybe getting to know her a bit better. He could hear the shower running on the verandah and he looked up as he crossed the newly-mown grass. A pink towel was hanging on the hook outside the door.

*Good. No funny business this afternoon. Keep it that way.*

Dominic put the beer on the table and walked down the stairs toward the back shed to see if their old boards were still in there. A grin crossed his face as Jilly's out of tune voice followed him down the steps as she sang in the shower.

*Shake your booty?* The picture that came to his mind kept the grin on his face. He'd never be able to look at Miss Henderson across the boardroom table again without thinking of her in a white bikini and shaking *her* booty.

Maybe he needed another cold shower. He'd turned the water down as cold as he could after he'd got back from the beach this morning, but it hadn't damped down the desire that had heated his blood since last night.

Opening the door of the old shed, he pushed aside the cobwebs and poked around until he came across the old kneeboards in the rafters. Still in their cloth bags and secured safely for ten years.

*Good on you, Derro.*

Dominic lifted the dark green board down—that one had been his favourite when he'd been learning to surf—and carried it up to the verandah; it was waxed ready to go. Strange that the wax hadn't dried up; must have been a good brand.

The singing had been replaced by a muttering and a strange rattling noise.

"Jilly? Are you okay?"

"No, I'm not. What the *fu* . . . what the heck are you playing at?"

He hurried along the verandah to the shower. The pink towel was still hanging on the hook. "Are you still in the shower?"

"Of course, I am. Now unlock the door and stop playing silly buggers."

Dominic stood outside the shower and rolled

his eyes. The bolt high on the outside of the shower door was drawn, effectively locking her in.

*How am I going to explain that?*

"Heh heh." The soft chuckle came from behind him and Dominic whirled around but of course there was nobody there.

"Stop laughing and unlock the door." Jilly was very unimpressed if the tone of her voice was any indication. He'd heard that exact tone when she'd been on the phone to the trading floor each time the share market fell.

He reached and up and slid the bolt open. "It's unlocked now, but Jilly, I swear I didn't lock it."

"So who did?"

"It must have jiggled its way along when you were singing?"

Dead silence.

"Go away, until I get out of here." Her voice was a bit softer. "Please, just go for a walk or something."

The door pushed open slowly and Dominic took off back to the shed. He would do as instructed.

Jilly's turn to be the boss.

# Chapter Eight

After she dried off in the bedroom, Jilly pulled on a clean pair of shorts and singlet top before she tied her purple sarong in a fancy twist around her neck, so it looked like a dress. Her temper was simmering; she was very unimpressed with Dominic's juvenile antics.

*What was his problem?* Nice to her face, and offering to take her for a surf?

Have a chat? Have a beer together? And then play stupid pranks on her?

So different to her serious boss from work. She shrugged before she ran a brush though her hair and twisted it up in a clip. He could come clean about the silly practical joke and they could laugh about it. All she wanted was honesty.

Staring at herself in the mirror, she frowned. If she was honest, she had to admit that the sight of Dominic was making her want more than that.

She ran a smudge of lip gloss across her lips before she stepped outside. He was at the far end of the porch watching the clouds swirl above the beach. The storm was building from the south and lightning lit the late afternoon sky. He turned as she walked along the wooden floor, her bare feet silent on the timber.

Jilly stood in front of him with her arms folded. He could talk first and explain what he was up to. He smiled but didn't speak.

She couldn't help herself. "So?"

The smile got wider, and irritation buzzed through her.

"So what?" he said. Was this guy really second-in-charge of a multi-billion-dollar trading bank?

"So what's with the teenage boy pranks? And while I'm saying my piece, I thought you'd agreed last night to stay out of my cottage while I was here."

This time Dominic frowned back at her. "What do you mean? I haven't been here today . . . not until now anyway. What pranks?"

"Like mow the lawn? And move my car?" Jilly leaned back against the verandah rail while she waited for him to answer, but all she got was a shake of his head. "And push my chair?" Her voice was softer now because she knew he couldn't have done that. He'd driven past a few seconds later.

He seemed to be thinking for a moment and Jilly narrowed her eyes waiting for his latest excuse.

"No. I've been in town."

"So who mowed the lawn?"

He shrugged. "My aunt organises the upkeep of the place. The handyman must have come while we were at the beach."

"On Christmas Day?"

He shrugged. "This is the north coast, not the city."

Her temper eased a little. "So, you didn't move my car and leave the house door open?"

"No. I didn't, and I wouldn't do that without checking with you." He smiled at her and the crinkles around his eyes made him look even sexier.

"Okay then . . . and you say the shower locked itself." Just as well he'd been here to get her out because there was no one else within calling distance and she would have been stuck in there.

"I'll have to prop it open next time I have a shower."

"I can hang around if you want to lock it." Dominic ran his hand through his hair and stared at her. Jilly's gaze dropped to his lips and a warm tremor ran through her as she remembered the dream she'd had about him. Followed instantly by heat flooding her cheeks.

He screwed his face up into a strange expression, opened his mouth, shook his head and then closed his mouth again. Jilly had never seen this confident man at a loss before. Finally, he ran his hand through his hair. "You *can't* stay here. I'm not going to say anymore because I don't want you to think I'm batshit crazy but—"

She waited for him to finish but Dominic held out his hand. "Come on. That beer's getting warm. We are going to have a Christmas drink and you can tell me a bit about yourself. Why you came up here for a holiday."

Jilly hesitated and then reached out and took his hand. Pleasant warmth tingled up her arm and headed south as he led her to the outdoor table and pulled out the chair. He popped the top of a beer and passed it to her, and she tipped it to her mouth, appreciating the cold liquid. The beer soothed her parched throat but the effect of one drink zinged through her whole body. She peeped from beneath half-closed lids as Dominic lifted his bottle, but he was looking at her. His gaze travelled slowly over her bare shoulders, down to the knot where her sarong was tied. It had been a long time since anyone had looked at her like that and a small thrill ran through her. She took another sip of beer; she needed to do something to ignore the rapid beat of her heat. She knew a flirtatious look; it might have been a long time between drinks, but she could read his mind.

"Not quite the Hilton where the firm held the

Christmas drinks." He smiled as she leaned back on the padded vinyl chair that was beneath the scarred wooden table. "I didn't see you there?"

A bolt of grief shot up from her chest and lodged in her throat. Jilly looked down at the table. The pre-Christmas function had been the same day as Dad's funeral. The girls couldn't understand why she wouldn't go, but she'd told no one about her Dad until she'd come back to work the day after the funeral. Finally, she lifted her head. "I was at a . . . a . . . funeral. I wasn't being anti-social."

"I'm sorry to hear that."

She lifted her head and he was looking curiously at her.

"You didn't miss much. A lot of silliness, too much drinking and some sore heads the next day."

"I heard how Shaz got Mr. Burns up on the dance floor.' She let out a little giggle. "Apparently he can tango with the best of them."

The ache in her throat eased as a sweet smile crossed Dominic's face. "The rose she put between his teeth was a nice touch."

"She's a mad character. Lightens the place up, doesn't she?" She was a good friend to Jilly, but despite that, Jilly didn't share much personal stuff with any of her work friends.

"She is. I often wonder why people let their hair down at work functions."

Jilly shrugged. "I know what you mean. Everyone is formal and on their best behaviour all year, and one night in the festive season can bring it all undone." She smiled at him ruefully. "And there speaks the voice of experience."

It was at last year's Christmas party that she'd met Phil's wife. That had been the last social work function she'd been to.

"You too?" Sympathy filled his expression. "I learned very early that work and pleasure don't mix." This time his laugh was rueful. "About ten years back, in my first position as a trader at the Federal Bank, I discovered too late that the lady who had me bailed up under the mistletoe was the chairman's wife."

Jilly relaxed as her laugh bubbled up. "I didn't know you worked at the Federal Bank."

He laughed with her. "I didn't after that. She told him I'd approached her!"

A serious note crept into her voice. "I worked there for a while too. It was an office romance that brought me undone too."

Dominic lifted his beer in the air. "Merry Christmas, Jilly. Here's to no office romances."

She lifted her beer and clinked the glass against his, ignoring the pang of regret that ran through her.

Dominic reached down to a bag on the floor. "I

199

almost forgot. I brought some dinner. Courtesy of the gas station." He pulled out a tin of smoked oysters, and some crackers and cheese. "I was going to suggest maybe cooking some steaks on the barbie, but the weather's put a stop to that."

Jilly uncurled her legs from beneath her and stood before disappearing into the kitchen. "I'll be back in a minute."

The smile that crossed Dominic's face when she put the plum pudding and custard in the middle of the table made the wait in the supermarket car park well worth it.

*Thanks, Ethel.*

"Merry Christmas to you too."

She sat back down and picked up her beer and watched as he traced his fingers over a scratch in the middle of the table. She leaned forward; DSP was scratched into the wood.

"So, you spent time here when you were growing up?" Jilly watched as his fingers moved across to another scratch. "Family house, you said?"

He looked up and held her eyes with his. "More than that. After my parents died, I grew up here at my grandparents' house. The one up the road where I'm staying. This one was Aunty Vi's." He jerked his head to the side. "Lived there till I left for uni."

"You?" Jilly pointed to the other initials near his. "Sisters and brothers?

"No, just me and my cousins." He picked up the oysters and peeled back the lid. "Two of them lived here and the other cousins who lived in Brisbane used to come and visit once a year. Christmas here was a busy and noisy time."

"Where are they all now?"

"Mostly scattered all over the world. And my grandparents passed on."

"I just lost my Dad." The words were out before she could think.

"So that's why you took some time off?"

She nodded mutely as the grief resurfaced.

"You should have taken longer." The kindness in his voice almost brought her undone and Jilly swallowed and changed the subject.

"It was what? Three days?" His gaze was fixed on her and she dropped her lashes and ran her finger around the rim of the bottle.

"Yeah, it was long enough. It's okay. But I might need the odd day to sort out the estate when we go back." Jilly sat back in her chair as he arranged the oysters next to the crackers and then passed the plate to her. "Thank you. And here I was thinking you were a city boy. Private school, old boys' network and all that."

He looked at her quizzically over his beer.

"Shouldn't make assumptions, should I?" She

lifted her beer and closed her eyes as she drank.

"What about you?"

"Guilty," she said. "Private school, uni and Dad's old boys' network got me the job at the bank."

"Everything you thought I was," he said with a quizzical look.

She nodded guiltily.

A comfortable silence settled between them and they sat back watching the storm come in over the sea. Jilly glanced at Dominic as he tipped his beer back and drank. He was wearing a shirt with the sleeves cut out. When he lifted his beer to his mouth, the muscles in his upper arm moved and Jilly couldn't help staring.

*For someone who spends all day in the office he looks pretty damn hot.*

A shaft of raw desire ran through her and she forced herself to look away, but not before she caught his gaze. Sweat dampened her brow and the skinny tank top she'd changed into after her shower clung to her chest. She looked down dismayed to see her nipples hard beneath the shirt. Lifting her eyes, heat ran through her; Dominic's eyes were at the same spot. She focused her attention on his lips. She'd never noticed how lush and kissable they were.

Jilly averted her eyes as she let out a shaky breath. For a moment, she'd thought he was going to lean over and kiss her. And it wouldn't have been unwelcome. Tension hovered in the air until he reached over and put his hand on top of hers on the table.

"Jilly—" The moment was broken as a sudden wind roared in from the ocean, accompanied by a loud crack of thunder. The hammock chair began to rock back and forth creaking loudly, and the shower door blew shut and the bolt slid across. The tension dissipated in a moment. They looked at each other and smiled.

"See, these things happen." Dominic stood and walked over to the shower and opened the lock. "All you need now is to find the person who mowed the lawn and I'm out of trouble." Those sexy lips opened in a wide grin and his white teeth flashed in the dimness that had descended as the black clouds raced in.

"I'll have to be more careful from now on." Jilly stood and walked across to the railing where he was leaning looking out to the storm. "I'm sorry. I do seem to be blaming you for everything that goes wrong." A low chuckle reached her, and she turned around with a frown. "What was that?"

"What?" Dominic looked around.

"That noise. Did you laugh?' The hair on

Jilly's neck stood to attention again—as did her nipples. Not that they'd ever gone down. She rubbed her arms, making out she was cold, nothing to do with this sexual attraction that was consuming her. As she let her gaze move up past those muscled arms to his sexy lips, she wondered how the hell she'd ever work next to him without combusting into a haze of lust.

He was just too damned good looking.

"Are you scared here by yourself?" Dominic leaned in closer to her and she got a whiff of surf, and sand, and sweaty man. She couldn't help taking a deep breath and inhaling the manly essence.

"No, why would you ask that?"

He shrugged. "It's pretty lonely out here. For a city girl."

"I'm fine. I'm enjoying the quiet." Jilly wasn't going to let him know how unsettled she was. It was only the storm that was bothering her. Not him or the spooky feeling that wouldn't go away. The old cottage took on a sinister air as more lightning flashed in from the sea.

"Are you still up for a surf in the morning?" Dominic pointed to the board propped up against the wall. "I found my old kneeboard in the shed. It's all waxed and ready to go."

"Will the weather be okay?"

"Guaranteed. This is just a summer storm."

Like the tumultuous feelings that were coursing through her as the touch of his hand warmed her skin. Her body was reacting to him with surprising heat. She lifted her drink and drained the beer, welcoming the fizz that coursed through her blood.

"For sure."

Another chuckle came from the dark and despite the heat of Dominic's body beside hers, goose bumps rose on her skin.

"Who was that?"

"Just the wind. Don't be nervous." His arm went around her, and he squeezed her shoulder and Jilly put aside her jumpiness.

Grow up, she chastised herself. He was right; this was a very different place to her apartment in Manly where there were people around day and night.

She swallowed as he kept his arm there; he was flirting with her and she didn't mind one bit. They weren't at work now; it was a vacation. Maybe she could put her rules aside for a day or two.

"I hope the weather's okay for our surf tomorrow. I'm looking forward to it." She shivered as the wind whipped around the verandah. "Do you want to come inside before this rain hits."

The cold breeze chilled her skin as Dominic stepped away. "It's time I went home." He'd put a barrier up suddenly. And his expression was back to that of Dominic, the boss. Was she giving out vibes he didn't want?

Jilly shrugged as she took a step back. Literally and emotionally. "What about the plum pudding?"

"Let's save it for after our surf tomorrow. You think I work you hard in the office, you ain't seen nothing yet. We'll get you working those waves." The distance had left his voice, but he moved towards the steps.

"Thanks for the beer. Do you want to take the rest back with you?"

"Nah." He waved dismissively. "Put them in your fridge. New Year's Eve is coming up."

"What time in the morning?" She kept her voice casual not wanting him to see her disappointment.

"Sunrise too early? Meet me on the beach."

Jilly nodded and with a final wave, Dominic disappeared into the darkness and emptiness surrounded her.

# Chapter Nine
*Boxing Day*

Despite the unsettled feeling that wouldn't leave Jilly as she sat on the lounge and read after a light dinner, she slept well. Before she went to bed, she double checked the locks on the window and the doors and left a light on in the kitchen. There was nothing she could do about the thin piece of lattice at the back of the kitchen that shook in the wind. She still couldn't shake the feeling that someone was watching her, which she knew was stupid, because there was no one within cooee.

Apart from Dominic. But one minute, he'd been up close and personal and then he'd withdrawn into himself and left in a matter of minutes.

The alarm on her iPhone roused her at 4.30 a.m. and she stumbled into the kitchen, rubbing her eyes, and reached for the kettle. Her hand froze on the tap as she looked up at the back door. *Unlocked and wide open.* And not only that, the surfboard that Dominic had left outside on the verandah was lying along the sofa, the cotton draw string bag that had encased it, lay scrunched on the rose-covered mat.

Jilly backed away and looked around.

"What the hell?" Her hands shook as she shut the back door and flicked the lock over. She'd forget about the cup of tea; just get changed and head to the beach.

Get out of this house. Forget about what Dominic said about it not being safe, being in here was beginning to creep her out a little.

The first rosy glimmers of dawn were streaking the sky with a soft apricot when she stepped outside, the board tucked beneath her arm. A warm wind puffed in off the hills this morning and everything had been washed clean from the storm last night. The wind must have blown the door opened, she reasoned to herself. And she must have carried the board inside when she was half-asleep and forgotten that she had. If she wasn't careful, she was going to have herself spooked and head home early, which she really didn't want to do. Sydney would be hot and busy, and she'd probably end up at work if she went home early.

Dominic tried to tell you not to stay here, a little voice nagged within her.

He was waiting for her on the beach, his strong,

muscular lines silhouetted by the rising sun behind him. The wet sand was smooth and shining, clear of footprints, as Jilly followed him to the water's edge.

"Sleep okay?" His eyes were hooded.

"Like a baby."

*Well, I did.*

"Good. Surf's great. You ready?" He waited for her to catch him up and they walked out into the water together until they were waist-deep. They waited for a break in the waves. When the last wave of the set broke and passed them with the white frothy foam bubbling around them, Dominic slid onto his board and lay on his stomach and began to paddle out into the deeper water. Anticipation filled Jilly as she waited for the next wave to pass. The rough wax on the board crumbled beneath her fingers as she gripped the sides with both hands and slid onto the length of the board. Before she could find her centre of balance, her bare stomach slid along the slippery board and she held on tight as the board slid away.

It was too late. The board bucked beneath her as the oncoming wave lifted the front of it and Jilly slipped off. She wasn't quick enough and gasped, copping a mouthful of saltwater as she went under the small wave that broke over her, and then carried the kneeboard into the shore.

It was a tossup whether embarrassment or

temper won out, and she let her temper build. That was the final straw. What the hell was Dominic playing at? Coughing and spluttering, she marched back through the shallows—as much as one could march in knee-deep water and stood at the edge of the sand, her arms folded as she waited for him to catch the next wave into shore.

*Of course* he did it gracefully, staying on the board until he was in knee-deep water.

"Are you okay? What happened?" He tossed his head back and his hair stuck to his neck. He reached up and brushed the long strands from his eyes.

Jilly glared up at him. "Just what is your problem? Do you really have to go to these extremes to get me to move out of your precious cottage? I suppose it was you who came back and left the door open last night when you brought the board inside, too?" Her words ran together as rage filled her chest.

The water splashed around Dominic's legs as he strode from the water. His mouth was tight, and his eyes were flashing as he put his board down carefully on the sand and turned to her.

"Would you like to tell me exactly how it's my fault that you fell off your board? I thought you said you could surf?"

Jilly let her temper burn ever hotter. She didn't

have red hair for nothing. She picked up the board and shoved it at him "When did you do that? In the middle of the night when I was asleep? You really do have a problem, don't you?"

Socializing and being pleasant to her boss was no longer an option after this prank. How the hell she was going to take him seriously enough to work with from now on was something she'd worry about when she went back to Sydney.

"I need this break and I'm not going to let you, or anyone else ruin it for me!"

She turned away, intending to leave him there, but stopped when Dominic reached out and held her arm. He held her firmly and took her board with his free hand. She saw the exact moment that he realised what she was upset about.

"Bloody hell," he said.

"Is that all you've got to say?" Jilly pulled her arm away and folded her arms. "Why on earth would you put soap on my board instead of wax?"

He put the board down on the ground and turned to her, his other hand holding her shoulder lightly. "I didn't." His eyes narrowed as he stared down at her. "And what was that you said about the door being open?"

"Don't worry about it. I'm going to go back, have a shower—and leave the door propped open while I have it—and have a peaceful day away from

211

you." She lifted her chin and held his gaze with hers. "So, are you going to let me go?"

Damn him. No matter how angry she was, Jilly had to admit how he really was irresistible. In a suit he'd looked fine, but standing in front of her, sun-drenched muscles, golden-chested and dripping with salt water, he was ridiculously handsome. Like some Greek god or something. She couldn't bear to think how much better he'd look without anything on at all. She blinked as she tried to clear the picture and the stupid comparisons from her mind. What the heck was wrong with her?

His chuckle was husky as he looked down at her. "I'm so sorry. I should have checked the board better." He reached up and tucked her hair behind her ear. "I'm really sorry. I'll stay out and you can have my board. I'll go back and get some wax."

Jilly shook her head, bemused as his eyes held hers. His touch was sending trembles down her back. "So, who soaped the board?"

Dominic stared down at her, his expression unreadable. "My cousin used to do it for a lark. He was the world's biggest practical joker."

Jilly picked up the sadness in Dominic's voice. "Was?" she asked quietly.

He lifted his gaze and pointed to the rocks on the point to the south. "Derro drowned on the point the day after his eighteenth birthday."

# Chapter Ten

Jilly's lips parted in sympathy as Dominic told her about Derro. He'd not spoken of the tragedy for years and his voice caught as he told her of waiting on the beach that afternoon; waiting hopelessly for Derro to reappear after he'd slipped beneath the water. But he hadn't.

"Luckily I had my phone and I called triple zero. The guys from the surf club in the next bay were here on the jet ski within minutes." He shook his head and lifted his gaze to the horizon. "It took two days for his body to wash up. His sister, Margaret found him. It was a pretty tough time for our family."

Jilly reached over and squeezed his hand. Dominic curled his fingers around hers and didn't let go.

They sat on the sand together as the sun

climbed quickly in the morning sky. He didn't tell her what was in his head, or a feeling within his heart; he had no proof and he didn't want to sound crazy.

"This is the first time I've had that board out since then, and he obviously had the last laugh. I suppose the soap dried up and as soon as it hit the water, it got slippery."

Last night he'd pulled back when she'd mentioned going inside. He knew she was attracted to him and he'd run. It was all too complicated; being her boss and the crazy situation at the beach cottage that he still couldn't get a handle on.

The sun caught her beautiful green eyes as she turned to him. His confusion dissipated like the spray above the waves as she steadily held his gaze. Instead of pulling away as he expected, she reached up and cupped his jaw in her hand.

"Forget about the board. Falling off didn't hurt me. I'm sorry about your cousin. It must have been so hard for you."

Dominic let go of her hand and put his arm around her shoulders. He didn't want her to move away. Her bare thigh was pressed up against his and what he wanted was only a breath away. He dipped his head, closed his eyes and lowered his mouth to hers.

Maybe it was a kiss returned because she felt

sorry for him—maybe not. All he knew was that her lips were sweet beneath his and he explored her mouth gently. She sighed his name and her breath whispered against his lips. Jilly reached up and her fingers tangled in his wet hair as she pulled him closer. There was more than sympathy in her response. He groaned against her mouth and pushed her gently back on the sand.

By the time he had kissed her lips, her face, and then slowly slid his lips down her neck to that sweet spot he had noticed in the shadow of her collarbone, she was arching against him. Dominic lowered his hand to slip it inside her bikini top and cupped her in his palm as she murmured with pleasure against his neck. He lifted his head and looked down at her, her eyes were wide; she looked more alive than he had ever seen her. Passion filled her eyes and a slow smile tilted those lips that had been against his neck a few seconds ago. The sharp bark of a dog brought him to his senses, and he pulled back and straightened her top.

He rolled over and sat up and looped his hands around his knees. Luckily the dog had run ahead and the couple walking along the beach was still a couple of hundred metres away. Jilly sat up and brushed the sand from her shoulders.

He stared out to sea, breathing deeply as the couple walked along the beach towards them.

Not a word was spoken.

***

Jilly folded her arms across her chest. Her heart was beating at the rate of knots and she flicked a glance at Dominic. He was staring out to sea; his jaw hard. His gaze steely. So many sensations ran through her; it was more than the physical. Somehow, she knew that they had connected on a deeper level than sheer physical need. If it hadn't been for the dog barking, they would have been making love. She craved his touch and shivered as he shifted his position and put more distance between them.

The dog bounded up to them, a huge black thing with floppy ears and loose jowls. She laughed as it nuzzled into her neck, the same place that Dominic's lips had been only minutes before. She jumped to her feet as the dog played around them, and she knew the exact second that Dominic turned to look at her, even though she wasn't watching him. She felt his eyes on her like a brand. It was crazy but she did.

The couple whistled to their dog and waved to Dominic and Jilly as they walked away.

"Do you want to go back in the surf on my board or go back to the cottage?"

She tried to read what was in his voice and subdue the restlessness that was in her. It was hard to quell, that deep ache low in her belly and the tingling down low made it hard to think logically.

She tried to lighten the mood. "How about some plum pudding for breakfast? It is Boxing Day."

His smile was distant and the warm feeling in her shrivelled. He'd started it and she'd made a fool of herself. Dominic stood and together they picked up their boards and headed back toward the cottages.

Her heart was still thudding in slow, heavy beats and the blood was zinging around her body. Her nerve endings were skittering all over the place as confusion filled her. But when they reached the road, Dominic turned to face her.

"Sorry the surfing was such a fiasco. We'll try again another morning, okay?" He hitched the board up higher and nodded at her. "Have a good day; I have to go to Coffs Harbour. Anything you need?"

Jilly shook her head. "No, thank you."

She watched him as he walked away, before she turned and went back to her place. This holiday was not working out how she'd planned. It was time to forget about Dominic and try to relax and have the rest she'd planned. It had been a long time since she'd made out on a beach, but the frustration that filled her had more to do with Dominic's hot and cold moods than any unfulfilled sexual needs.

## ##

The day passed slowly. No matter how much Jilly tried to push him from her mind, Dominic wouldn't leave her thoughts. She'd come here for the quiet and today, she got in—in bucket loads. She read and dozed and took herself off for a long walk down to Valla Beach after lunch. Burned off the chocolate, the strawberry milk and the beer. The cottage up the road stayed quiet and empty and there was no sign of Dominic's silver car.

When she came back from her walk, she settled gingerly in the hammock chair with a cold drink and her Kindle. She looked around nervously as she plumped up the cushions. No wind this afternoon. She pushed her foot onto the floor and rocked the chair gently as she began to read.

"Who the hell are you?"

Jilly dropped her Kindle with a start and slid out of the hammock as a woman clumped up the wooden steps. She strode along the verandah towards her, arms swinging wildly by her sides. It was hard to pick her age; her skin was tanned a deep nut-brown and her face was set in a ferocious glare. Her hair was looped up in some sort of old-fashioned beehive bun, she wore a pair of men's boardshorts and a bikini top and her feet were bare and encrusted with dirt. One hand pointed at Jilly, in the other was a small garden spade which she was now waving around.

Before Jilly could reply, she was hit with another spray of angry words. "What the hell are you doing in my brother's house?"

Jilly straightened and took a step back as the garden spade came perilously close to her head. The woman's dark eyes were fixed intently on her.

"I'm Jilly Henderson and I'm renting this house for the Christmas break."

"Says who?" The woman stepped closer.

"Says me. And I believe you are trespassing." Jilly lifted her chin as anger replaced fear. "Unless you can be civil, perhaps you should leave."

"No. I've come to weed the garden." She took a step back and pointed to the overgrown garden bed along the front fence.

Jilly's eyes narrowed. "Was it you who mowed the lawn yesterday."

"Yes, and I suppose it was your car that was in the way." Even though her face was unfriendly the woman had lowered her voice. "I washed my feet before I moved it.

Well at least that let Dominic off the hook. He *had* been telling her the truth all along.

"Was it you who left me the flowers? On the kitchen table?"

"No. I didn't leave them for you. They were for

my brother."

"Your brother?"

"Yes, Derek. I guess he was the one who organised the rental. I'm sorry for intruding. I'll leave the garden till you move out. How long are you here?"

"Another three days."

"Okay. Sorry to bother you, Jilly. I'm Margaret." She gave a shrill laugh as she went back down the steps and opened the gate. "They call me mad Margie but don't believe a word they say."

Jilly watched as Margaret strode along the road until she disappeared around the corner. This was the strangest vacation she had ever taken.

Maybe Vanuatu would have been more peaceful.

Although there'd be no Dominic there.

## 

She showered early and dressed with care, blow-drying her hair into loose curls, wondering if—hoping—Dominic might come over for another sunset chat. She peered into the oval, cracked mirror above the small vanity in the outside toilet. Her skin had a healthy glow and the dark circles beneath her eyes had faded. Despite the unexpected and interesting events over the past couple of days, she was finally managing to relax.

The evening was cool; not a breath of wind disturbed the air tonight. Jilly sat on the steps of the verandah and enjoyed the peaceful setting as the sun set over the she-oaks. A rain bird called mournfully from the bush and then all was quiet. Dominic's house was in darkness and she thought back to the interlude on the beach this morning. They'd both made a mistake, not giving any thought to the conversation when they'd both agreed that work flings were definitely a no-go zone. Hopefully, they'd both put it behind them and forget about the kiss at the beach when they were back in the office.

Gradually the dark crept in and Jilly stood slowly, ignoring the regret that filled her. A soft southerly wind puffed in off the ocean and her sarong wound around her legs as the breeze lifted it.

She shook her head. Sheer pleasure had filled her when Dominic had put his lips on hers and she wasn't going to regret one second of it. For the first time in many months she felt alive and if he was happy to spend some time with her, she'd welcome him into her life. They were two grownups and surely they could handle some time together out of work. The way Dominic had kissed her—and touched her—this morning, she knew he was interested. If it hadn't been for that dog…

It *was* lonely here by herself and she would enjoy his company again. Opening the fridge, she carried some salad leaves inside and sat at the table listening for his car.

But nothing.

Finally, after a light meal she changed into her PJs and climbed into bed. She hadn't even heard his car come back when she fell asleep just before midnight. The only sound was the soft sighing of the waves through the trees as they washed up on the beach.

When Jilly woke with a start it was pitch dark. She lay there for a moment listening and wondering what had woken her. She shivered; there was a chill in the room. Goose bumps rose on her bare skin and the hair on the back of her neck lifted. Her mouth dried as the other side of the bed dipped and she rolled toward the centre of the bed.

She tensed as a hand crept onto her hip.

"Dominic?" Her throat was dry, and the words came out raspy and sleepy.

"Heh heh." The same soft chuckle she had heard on the verandah turned her blood to ice.

Pulling all her courage together, she swallowed and reached over. Taking a deep breath and trying to stay calm she placed her hand on the warm fingers that still rested lightly against her hip.

"Who are you?" She pulled the shaky words from that nervous place in her chest at the same time she pushed her fingernails into the hand now holding her firmly. The man chuckled again, and the bed dipped again as he rolled away. Jilly rolled over in one fluid movement and was on her feet, reaching for the light before she could even draw a breath. She clicked the switch, bathing the room in bright white light, and she looked around for something to use as a weapon.

There was no one in the room with her and the door was still shut. Drawing in a shaky breath, she walked around to the other side of the bed and bent down, looking underneath.

*Nobody. Nothing.* The only thing in the room was a chill that raised the goose bumps on her arms. Jilly grabbed a blanket off the bed and backed into the chair in the corner, her eyes fixed on the door in front of her.

\*\*\*

Dominic came in late, his thoughts churning. Kissing Jilly at the beach had been a stupid thing to do; it had been her sympathy and wide eyes that had weakened him to her charms. God, if it hadn't been for that slobbery dog, he probably would have ripped her white bikini off and made love to her on the sand. His hard and fast rule of non-involvement at work would have been broken irrevocably because he knew once he had a taste of making love to Jilly, there was no way he'd be able to hold back.

223

He had to work with her, and he was not going to get involved with someone at the office.

Mr. Iceberg he would stay. He knew the nickname the girls had given him, and it suited him just fine. But the feel of Jilly's breast beneath his hand and the taste of her salty skin on his lips had stayed with him all day. Not trusting himself to keep his hands off her, he'd gone for a long drive, telling himself he was simply checking out the surf up the coast.

A stupid move; he'd got caught in the Boxing Day traffic and had been held up on the highway until well after dark. The other cottage was in darkness and he guessed Jilly was asleep when he finally drove past, resisting the temptation to call in and check on her.

Three more days; he'd keep his distance and when they were back in Sydney, nothing would be changed and there'd be no messy holiday romance to get over.

That's what his head told him anyway; his heart was saying something different as the blood hammered though his body. Another cold shower was in order.

After he parked the car, he pushed open his own front door in disgust and threw the keys onto the table. He went to bed and tossed and turned until a restless sleep over took him.

# Chapter Eleven

*December 27*

In the early dawn, the southerly wind strengthened, and the bathroom door clicked on and off its latch until Dominic couldn't put up with it any longer. He yawned and sat on the edge of the bed rubbing his eyes.

"Tired, mate?"

The familiar voice hit Dominic in the gut. He dropped his hands and slowly lifted his head. Derro was lounging back in the chair beside the bed, smiling at him, his tanned face crinkled around the eyes so like his own.

*Hell.* Dominic rubbed his eyes again.

His cousin, his *dead* cousin, sat in the chair dressed in his familiar faded denims and favourite Metallica T-shirt. They'd gone to that concert in Sydney for Dominic's eighteenth birthday. Derro took a bite from the apple he was holding. The sweet smell of the juice drifted over to Dominic along with the loud crunch.

"Don't stress. It's cool."

*Crunch,* as he bit the apple again.

"Derro?" Dominic's voice was a ragged whisper. "Shit, I'm dreaming, aren't I?"

"Nup, no dream. It's me, man."

The familiar grin tore at Dominic's chest and he took a deep breath. "Really?"

The cheeky nod he knew so well confirmed it.

"Yeah. I've been keeping an eye out for you and you're sure stuffing things up."

"What? Where?"

"Are you really happy being a suit, Dom?" Derro stood and walked around the table and pegged the apple core into the bin.

*Do ghosts eat apples? Or am I dreaming?*

Dominic stood and resisted pinching himself. He looked down at the bed. He wasn't lying there asleep. He was awake and talking to his dead cousin.

"Shit, Derro. Why did you have to go and drown? Do you know how much I missed you?"

"It was my time, Dom. But I had to come back and sort you out before I can move on. Couldn't let you stuff up too."

"What happened?"

Derro's face split into a wide grin. "Caught the best wave of my life, man. A six-foot left hander on the point. Perfect tube, but I didn't pull out in time."

Dominic shook his head, still unable to believe what he was seeing and hearing.

"So enough about me. I'm fine. I'm here to give you a bit of advice."

Dominic stared at his cousin. "Advice?" He cleared his throat and the words rasped out.

"Don't let her go. Don't let that stupid career, and figures and money drive your life. Jilly's the one for you, mate. I used Margie's email to set up the rental. That was interesting." He walked to the window and turned back to Dominic. "I've done my best to throw you together, but it's up to you now. You have to decide what *you* want."

Dominic knew what he wanted, and it had nothing to do with suits and the trading floor. Derro smiled at him as he read his expression; he knew him well and always had.

"Good." Derro turned back to Dominic. "Want to go for a surf later? I'll be out there with you if you go."

Dominic's throat ached and he blinked as a sheen of moisture misted his eyes. "I wish."

"Look out for Margie, mate. Tell her I'm okay. She's still doin' it tough too." Derro walked over and grabbed him in a tight man hug. "Have a good life, Dom."

Gradually the pressure of his arms lessened,

and Dominic opened his eyes. The room was empty, and he looked around.

"What the hell?" he muttered as he flopped onto the bed and put his hands over his eyes. He leaned back onto the soft pillow and closed his eyes as the wind rattled around the house.

A persistent banging at the door woke him a couple of hours later. The dream had been so real; he still carried the same sense of loss in his chest that he'd experienced when Derro had left him.

*Maudlin.* That's what he was. Dreaming of the past. Time to go back to the city and his real life. Dominic rolled out of bed and had the door open before he was properly awake. Jilly stood there, her face pale and dark shadows beneath her eyes.

"Hi, come on in."

She stepped past him without speaking, and stood there looking at him, before she brushed a shaky hand over her face. She was dressed in a cute pair of pyjamas and he raised his eyebrows.

"You are going to think I am so crazy, but this really strange thing happened to me last night." Her voice was soft and her green eyes wide as she stared up at him

"You're not Robinson Crusoe." Calm settled over Dominic as he looked her. Derro—or his dream—whatever it had been, had given him a

228

choice. He put his hands on her shoulders, surprised to feel her trembling. "So shush, and listen to me. I'm sorry I was such a grouch yesterday and took off and left, but you scare me."

"Scared? Tell me about it."

"What's wrong?" Her skin was silky against his fingertips as he ran them down her arms.

"I was frightened last night, too."

Dominic groaned and he narrowed his eyes. "Don't tell me you had a dream too?"

"No, I had a flesh and blood visitor. I thought it was you, until he chuckled. And then he disappeared." Jilly's eyes were wide. "I was so scared I spent the rest of the night sitting up in a chair. I don't know what it was but there was definitely someone in the house."

"Just give me a moment." Dominic crossed to the kitchen and lifted the top of the bin. He shook his head as disbelief ran through him; a fresh apple core lying at the bottom of the plastic-lined bin. Maybe he'd put it there without remembering?

He turned back to Jilly and took her arm gently before leading her over to the bed. "You do look tired. Do you want to go back to bed? Get some sleep?" He grinned at her as her eyes locked with his. Enough of the stuffed shirt businessman. Dominic, the wild surfer without any worries, had come roaring back.

*Thank you, coz.*

From now on, the risks he took would have nothing to do with trades and shares. He sat on the edge of the bed and held his arms out and could have sworn he heard a chuckle as Jilly sat on his knee.

"Shut the door on the way out, Derro," he said quietly.

##

Certain that Dominic would hear the thudding of her heart Jilly leaned into him as his arms went around her waist.

"Back to bed? Here?" Her voice was tentative. "You're not going to go all cold on me again?"

A warm feeling suffused her as a rumble of laughter vibrated against her chest. "No, trust me. I had a very good lesson through the night." She frowned as he glanced over to the bin. "Mr. Iceberg's gone for good this time."

This time the heat was from embarrassment and she pulled back and stared at him. "How did you know that's what they call you at work?"

Dominic laughed again. "I wondered if you knew that the walls between my office and the staff room are very thin." He bent his knee and waggled his foot in the air in front of them. "That Shaz has some interesting theories."

Jilly stared at him, the heat in her face warring for supremacy with the heat that was building in her girlie parts. "You hear everything?"

"Everything." His lips zoomed in on her warm neck and her breath caught in her throat.

Choking out a strangled laugh, she shivered as his fingers slid down and held the bottom of her pyjama top. "Oh my God, how embarrassing!"

"But you, Miss Henderson, are always most circumspect in your conversations with your work friends." He tipped his head to the side with raised eyebrows and Jilly nodded. She closed her eyes as the soft cotton brushed her face when he lifted the top over her head.

"Are you sure?" He leaned forward and nuzzled his lips into her neck

Confidence surged through Jilly and she gave him a wicked smile. "I guess I won't be sure Mr. Iceberg has really gone unless you share some body heat with me."

Jilly couldn't help the small giggle that escaped as she looked down at his feet. He lifted his head. "What?"

"Nothing." She shook her head. "Just testing out a theory or two."

"And?"

Again, a little giggle. "You do have big . . .

feet."

"I aim to please." Dominic lifted her off his lap and laid her on the bed. Jilly lay there admiring the play of the muscles in his thighs as he bent down. She closed her eyes.

*God, was this a dream too?* If it was, she was going to enjoy every moment of it. A snap of foil and he was back beside her, the warmth of his skin against her body heating her from shoulder to toe.

Unfamiliar emotion flooded her. "Definitely not Mr. Iceberg," she murmured.

**

Dominic knew he'd remember the little sounds coming from Jilly's lips for the rest of his life. He cupped her hips, loving the feel of her soft curves against him.

"Warm enough now?" he murmured against her neck. He kissed her shoulder and traced his lips to the nape of her neck.

"Not an iceberg to be seen," she said with a sexy giggle.

He fell asleep with Jilly's legs wrapped around his, holding him close.

# Chapter Twelve

*New Year's Eve*

Jilly rolled over and propped her head on her elbow. Dominic was sleeping peacefully beside her, his broad chest rising gently with his breathing. She had moved her few things into his cottage when he'd locked up his cousin's cottage three days ago. She reached out and tucked a stray curl behind his ear, but he didn't stir. The last few days had been wonderful. She'd done more wild things with him this week than she had in her whole life. Beach sex. Up against the wall sex. Morning Sex. Afternoon sex and one all night marathon session. Luckily Dominic had filled his fridge with groceries because her appetite was insatiable. Not only for him, but for food as well.

*Eating, sleeping, surfing, and sex. A magic vacation.* She grinned to herself—maybe magic wasn't the right word to use. He'd driven into town and brought his cousin Margaret back for lunch on their second last day. Margie was quirky but friendly to Jilly, especially once she knew that

Derro's cottage was empty again. She'd bolted down her lunch and borrowed a garden spade from Dominic's shed, preferring to weed the garden than catch up on old times with her cousin and his—

*His what?* Jilly wondered.

*His executive assistant? His girlfriend? His lover?* A quiver of uncertainty ran through her as she wondered what things would be like when they returned to Sydney.

All doubts fled when Dominic opened his eyes and reached for her. His lips found hers before she could speak but Dominic said all there was to say without words.

##

"How do you want to greet the New Year?" Dominic came up behind her in the kitchen as she washed some lettuce leaves in the old sink. "Mary at the servo tells me there's a rocking party at the river."

"What river?"

His deep laugh sent a shiver though her. She'd fallen hard for this man over the past few days. Working with him for the last six months, although distant, had already shown her what a good man he was. He was a man of integrity, kind and considerate. This week had also shown her what a great sense of humour he possessed . . . and what a versatile lover he was.

"The one around the point."

"Didn't know there was one. You've barely let me out of bed."

"Are you complaining, Miss Henderson? Am I working you too hard again?"

"I'm not. But tonight's our last night before we go back to the big smoke and I think I'd rather stay in unless you want to go out?" She turned around and held his gaze steadily. "What's going to happen when we go back to work? What about our rules?"

"I've had an idea and our rules aren't going to matter." Jilly looked up at him, but he wouldn't be drawn into discussing his idea.

He shook his head. "Come on, we'll head into the shops and get some food and I'll cook you a fabulous meal. Tempt you with some local seafood, perhaps?"

"Tempt me? I don't need seafood for that. Maybe some whipped cream and strawberries? What do you think of that?" she said in a husky voice.

"Mm. Maybe ice cream? Your skin is feeling very hot."

They made the local shops five minutes before closing time.

\*\*\*

235

Rested and relaxed, Dominic and Jilly packed his Audi ready for the trip back to Sydney together later that afternoon. For some reason, her car was stone dead and she knew Dominic suspected that a well-meaning—but ghostly—hand had been at work. He had insisted that they needed to have a midday nap to prepare for the trip ahead, but of course very little sleep had taken place. She shook her head and her hair brushed against his shoulder, but his eyes remained closed as his chest rose and fell gently.

If anyone had told her the events that would pass when she came for her solitary holiday at the beach, she would have told them they had had a touch of sun, or perhaps too much Christmas cheer. But Dominic's explanation had been heartfelt and had supported the things that had happened to her over the past few days; Jilly wondered whether a ghostly influence really had been at work bringing them together. Or was it simply that their deepest desires had culminated in dreams that had guided their choices.

She would never forget that night of terror sitting up in the chair when something had frightened her out of the cottage and into Dominic's arms. She moved to lie back on her pillow, but her hand was held and pressed against a tanned and golden-haired chest. She sighed and smiled into the wicked eyes that were holding hers and she gave into the exquisite sensation that ran through her whenever he touched her. Anywhere, anytime— even a touch on her back as he walked behind her sent shimmers of desire running straight through her. She let out a little giggle.

"What's so funny?" Dominic's fingers were doing wicked things to Jilly's composure as they moved down her back. She rolled over and lay on top of him.

She smiled at him and kept her tone saucy. "I was just thinking about the size of your feet and whether I should tell Shaz about her theory."

"Don't you dare." His voice was husky as he moved his lips down the side of her neck.

"I'll be able to tell the girls that I have tested the theory and that Mr. Iceberg has a new nickname. Mr. Hot Stuff, maybe?" She giggled at the look on his face as he pulled her down to his chest.

"Oh, I don't think so, Miss Henderson. I think you'll be doing exactly what your boss says."

And Jilly did for the next hour or two.

## 

"I've got a proposition for you," Dominic said later that afternoon.

Jilly threw him a laughing glance. "We don't have time."

"I'm serious." He walked across to her.

She tilted her head to the side. His face was closed, and he looked more like Dominic the boss. Zipping up her toiletries bag, she put it on the bed and walked across to him. She slipped her arms around his waist, revelling in her new-found ease with this man.

"Tell me."

"How much do you like living in Sydney?"

"I don't. I'd be out of there like a shot if I could get a decent job out of the city."

"How would you like to be my executive assistant in another business? Out of the city?"

Hope flowed through her as she stared up at him.

"Where?"

"How about here? We can do what we do from anywhere, you know. There's more to life than work and with our experience, we could work from here and use our skills consulting and telecommuting in the finance industry."

"And surf some of the day?"

A slow grin crossed his face as she looked up at him and saw her expression.

"Amongst other physical activities."

In the end they decided to leave Jilly's car there; it was a good excuse to come up for another weekend and start to set up their home office until they were replaced at the bank. Dominic's Audi was packed with their bags, and both surfboards were secured to the roof racks.

"We'll have to surf at Narrabeen until we move back," he said. "You can't let all that surfing practice go to waste." He locked the front door of the cottage and walked slowly along the verandah. Jilly waited for him in the car and he smiled as she caught his eye.

"Hurry up. It's hot in the car." She waved a hand in front of her face in an exaggerated movement. "Come on and get those big feet walking over here, boss."

Dominic smiled back at her. "Whatever you say, Miss Henderson."

Dominic had no doubt that in some way, Derro—whether it had been a dream or not—had shown him the way to where his future and true happiness lay.

*With Jilly. At the beach.*

He slipped into the driver's seat and started the car. Slowly he drove down the driveway and glanced in the rear-view mirror, back at the cottage where he had spent many happy years, and where he was going to make a life with Jilly. He touched her hand and gestured back behind them.

Though the haze of the late afternoon, Derro leaned against the fence, his surfboard beneath his arm. Lazily, he lifted his arm and waved before he turned and walked across the sandy road to the beach, disappearing into the sea mist that hadn't been there a moment before.

THE END

*I hope you've enjoyed these two Christmas stories*

*Turn the page for other books and series by Annie.*

# Other Books from Annie

Whitsunday Dawn
Undara
Osprey Reef

## Porter Sisters Series

Kakadu Sunset

Daintree

Diamond Sky

Hidden Valley

Larapinta

## Pentecost Island Series

Pippa

Eliza

Nell

Tamsin

Evie

Cherry

Odessa

Sienna

Tess

Isla


**The Augathella Girls Series (2022)**
Outback Roads (February)
Outback Sky (April)
*Plus more to follow*


**Sunshine Coast Series**

Waiting for Ana

The Trouble with Jack

Healing His Heart

Sunshine Coast Boxed Set


**Bondi Beach Love Series**

Beach House

Beach Music

Beach Walk

Beach Dreams

The House on the Hill


**Second Chance Bay Series**

Her Outback Playboy

Her Outback Protector

Her Outback Haven

Her Outback Paradise

The McDougalls of Second Chance Bay
Boxed Set

**Love Across Time Series**

Come Back to Me

Follow Me

Finding Home

The Threads that Bind

**Others**

The Trouble with Paradise

Deadly Secrets

Adventures in Time

Silver Valley Witch

The Emerald Necklace

Worth the Wait

Ten Days in Paradise

www.ingramcontent.com/pod-product-compliance
Lightning Source LLC
Chambersburg PA
CBHW020404120726
47904CB00002B/705